Up To No Good

MARG MCALISTER

BLUE GEM PUBLISHING

This edition published by Blue Gem Publishing in 2022.

Title: Up to No Good | Marg McAlister, author

ISBN: 978-1-922772-31-2 (Paperback edition)

ISBN: 978-0-9945205-3-1 (Ebook edition)

Cover Design by Annie Moril

V04032022

ALSO BY MARG McALISTER

SERIES 1
Good to Go

Georgie Be Good

Good Riddance

Up to No Good

In Good Hands

Too Good to be True

As Good as It Gets

Good Golly Miss Molly

Good Vibrations

A Rocking Good Christmas

SERIES 2
Good Intentions

A Good Result

No Good Reason

Good Fortune

CHAPTER 1

A Special Event

Georgie sat with her chin resting on her hand, frowning at her crystal ball. She should have been a hacker instead of a fortuneteller. Hackers could dig deep and find out people's deepest, darkest secrets with much more certainty than staring into a stupid crystal ball.

Being a wizard could work, too. *Schazam*, wave a wand and demand answers from… well, somebody. Or maybe to have messages from beyond arrive via owl post, like Harry Potter.

"Will I marry and have children?"

"Give me a second; an owl will be along any second now with the answer."

She reached over and smoothed a hand over the gleaming surface of the crystal ball and then gave it a light tap. "Come *on*. What's going on with you?"

For two weeks now, her crystal ball had been acting up—if that was the correct term to use with something that didn't plug into a wall. Her customers still seemed entertained enough—but there was some kind of severe blockage in the channel.

Did you even *call* it a channel?

Georgie groaned and banged her head gently on the table. She was such a know-nothing. A couple of months of success had made her over-confident; that was the problem. She had expected her understanding of all this to grow, and instead, she had gone backward. So much for being an eighth-generation gypsy who had supposedly inherited the Sight.

What had happened to the strange drifting white mist that had scared her to death the first time she used the crystal ball? It was gone. *Gone.* She needed it; it had always presaged some sort of insight.

Light footsteps sounded on the steps outside her trailer, and Layla's cheerful voice called, "Georgie?" before she appeared in the doorway.

"Hi," Georgie said without enthusiasm.

Layla took in the situation at a glance. "It's still not working, huh?"

"No. I'd ask Rosa what's going on, but I can't

bother her right now." Her great-grandmother had used the crystal ball for decades before Georgie, so should know its quirks, but a few days earlier, Rosa had taken a tumble down the steps of one of the new gypsy trailers back at the Johnny B. Goode RV Empire. With a sprained ankle and a nasty knock to the head, she was resting up in bed. According to Georgie's father, she was covered in bruises and more temperamental than ever.

"How is she?" Layla set down the folders she was carrying on the table and slid into the opposite seat. "It can't be good news for a ninety-year-old lady to have a fall like that."

"The doc says she's in amazing shape for someone her age but was lucky not to break a hip. He's ordered bed rest for another week, and she's not happy about it."

"Good thing you're two hundred miles away," Layla said. She jerked a thumb at the folders. "Do you want to go through sales figures now or leave it for tomorrow?"

Georgie eyed the folders, feeling guilty for not showing more interest. Layla was doing a brilliant job selling vintage trailers. Not only that, she had an entrepreneurial eye for what the retro crowd wanted. A vintage trailer was just the first step: they wanted to play house with it after that. Dress it up, buy things for it, buy clothes for themselves to look the part… even now, she could hear the happy beat of rock and roll hits of the 50s somewhere outside, where the rockabilly band booked for the retro rally was in full swing. She owed it to Layla to spend some time on this.

"No, let's do them now." She gently covered up the crystal ball with the familiar black velvet cloth, almost as though tucking a sick child into bed.

That made her think of Rosa lying in her bed, and she flicked a glance at Layla. "Do you think that there's any connection between Rosa's accident and what's going on with the crystal ball?"

Layla widened her eyes at her. "You're asking *me*?"

"Well, I was just thinking…she had it forever before she passed it on to me, and now it's playing up just as she has an accident." Georgie thought about it some more. "I know the problems started *before* her accident, but it can see the future, right?"

"Not exactly, from what I've seen. *You* see the future, using it as a conduit." Then Layla shrugged. "I'm just guessing. I don't have a clue."

"Nor do I." Deciding to leave her uncooperative crystal ball to its own devices, Georgie moved it to its place on the shelf. "What have we got?"

Layla flipped open a folder. "Overall sales figures for vintage trailers are still climbing. Your dad made the right call; there are plenty of people out there who want the retro look without restoration problems. Our vintage renovation team of specialists is growing too. People find it's too hard to do it themselves and end up coming to us." She turned the folder around so Georgie could read the numbers.

Georgie skimmed through the figures, and her eyebrows rose. "Nothing like the figures for motorhomes and fifth wheels, of course, but this is enough to keep Dad happy. Jerry too, now that he's finally let Tammy put vintage trailers near the entrance instead of hogging all the space for his precious motorhomes." She and Layla exchanged a grin. It was a source of enjoyment to both of them to see Georgie's conniving brother Jerry being deftly outmaneuvered by his retro-look girlfriend. Jerry, it seemed, had, at last, met his match.

"Speaking of Jerry," Layla said, "have you *seen* your brother today?"

"Not since breakfast."

"You know how Tammy's been all mysterious about a surprise? Well, I just spotted him ducking back inside her trailer. All I can say is, he doesn't look like the usual Jerry."

"Ye-es…?" Georgie made 'give it up' motions with her fingers.

"Tammy has sworn me to secrecy. Just know that you don't want to miss this." Layla mimed zipping her lips and sat back with a gleam in her eye.

"Miss what?"

"A special event at 3 pm."

Georgie eyed her suspiciously, and then her jaw dropped. "They're not going to announce their *engagement*, are they?"

"No, no." Layla hastily waved away that idea. "Nothing like that. I can't say any more. Just make sure you're in front of the stage at three o'clock."

Georgie glanced at her watch, cunningly disguised as a gorgeous gypsy bracelet. "That's only twenty minutes away."

"So let's run through these. Won't take long." Swiftly, Layla summed up the current orders and the production schedule and finished up with a list of prospects. Then she grinned. "Now for the fun stuff: our spinoff lines. Tammy has started an eBay store for retro chinaware, flatware, kitchen acces-sories, cushions, and posters. She's got ideas for more—see here?" Her finger skated down a list. When Georgie nodded, she flipped to the next section. "Here we have the clothing line. There's your Gypsy Georgie label, and here's Tammy's line of 50s fashions. She's going to add the 40s and 60s as well, but this is a start."

Georgie shook her head, smiling. "Who would have thought this would grow so big?"

"I know." Layla gave a happy sigh.

"Jerry might make more money with his extreme RVs," Georgie said, "but we have more fun." The thought of Jerry made both of them check the time.

"Let's go." Layla slid out of the seat and ran down the steps, with Georgie close on her heels, careful not to catch a heel in her gypsy skirt. Whatever it was that had Layla so excited, it sounded as though it would be worth seeing.

CHAPTER 2

He's Up to Something...

"Perfect timing—look, the band's just finishing a set," Layla called over her shoulder, weaving her way through the crowd.

"Excuse me…" Georgie squeezed through in her wake, edging past a group of thirty-somethings in bobby sox and bright dresses and men with t-shirts under black leather jackets. She and Layla finally snagged a spot close to the stage.

The MC tapped the mic a couple of times, made an expansive gesture toward the band, and boomed: "Weren't they great, folks? Let's hear it: give it up one more time for Rockabilly Fillies!"

The revved-up crowd cheered and whistled while the all-girl band punched the air and then moved their mic stands back to make room at the front of the stage.

"And now," the MC said, "we have something exceptional. A girl who was one of our finalists in the rock'n'roll comp last year, a talented singer and dancer… I'm sure you all know Tammy Dyson, who runs the Vintage and Retro Division at the Johnny B. Goode RV Empire. C'mon up, Tammy!"

More yells and cheers as Tammy skipped up the steps, quickly followed by ear-splitting wolf-whistles from a good number of the males present.

"Oh wow," Georgie said. Tammy took her breath away. She always looked terrific, but today, clad in black spandex pants and a tight off-the-shoulder black top, she was stunning. Her blonde hair fell in an artfully-styled tumble of curls around her face. "She's Sandy from Grease!"

Tammy pranced about a bit on the stage and waved to the crowd, looking perfectly steady in her high-heeled bright red shoes, to a shrill chorus of deafening whistles.

The MC had to hold up a hand and call for quiet before he could go on. "And appearing with Tammy is someone else you know all know well, someone who's had a hand in designing half the trailers here today…Jerry B. Goode!"

Jerry bounded up to join Tammy, and Georgie's mouth dropped open. "That's *not* Jerry!" She spared a moment to shoot a bemused glance at Layla, who was waiting for her reaction with a huge grin.

"Told you it was a don't-miss." Layla returned her attention to the stage.

"But Jerry has never in his life dressed in retro. *Never.*"

"He wasn't besotted with Tammy before," Layla pointed out.

Georgie stared at her brother, the Danny Zuko half of the equation. His hair was smoothed back and swept up into a quiff at the front, and his gym-honed body looked incredible in a tight black t-shirt and black pants. He looked alarmingly sexy and dangerous.

"The question is," Layla muttered, "Can he dance?"

"He can, actually," Georgie confirmed absently, watching her brother sling an arm around Tammy's shoulders and blow kisses to cheering faces upturned to watch the show. "He tells me it's an invaluable aid to picking up women."

"Sounds like Jerry," Layla said, and then added, "Come to think of it, there wasn't much dancing in that video clip anyway. As long as he can act."

That made Georgie laugh. "Jerry's done noth-ing *but* act from the time he was in diapers. It's an essential skill for a schmoozer like him."

The band played the opening few bars to *You're the One that I Want*, and Jerry walked over to the side of the stage to stand with his back to Tammy, feigning ignorance of her presence. She winked at the audience and then set her hands on two trim hips while she eyed his back.

Laughing, Layla and Georgie joined in the cheers and clapped to the beat.

Tammy walked over to tap Jerry on the shoulder, and he whirled, his eyes widening dramatically at the sight of her. The music swelled, and the crowd roared in anticipation.

Watching the song unfold, Georgie could scarcely believe this was her brother. She'd seen him in camo gear with his preppers; she'd seen him in a tux; she'd seen him in smart casual. She'd never seen him looking as though he should be racing hot rods with the bad boys from the 50s.

And, dammit, *this* look suited him as much as anything else.

Layla leaned over and yelled in her ear, *"And the legend grows!"*

Georgie nodded. Exactly. Jerry already had a massive profile among the RVing community, and this would make him the darling of the retro set as well. With the lovely Tammy kicking up her heels by his side, he would be unstoppable.

Tammy and Jerry pranced about the stage, Tammy singing her part and Jerry miming his. When they finished, the applause took a full minute to die down. They hugged and kissed and obligingly held a few poses for the cameras. Then Jerry jumped down, turned around, and theatrically held out his arms for Tammy to leap into, which she did flawlessly.

"One more before the break?" Jerry yelled up to the band, with Tammy in his arms. They gave a thumbs-up and, to the crowd's delight, launched straight into *Greased Lightnin'*.

"I'm there!" squealed Layla and threw herself into the gyrations with some of her cronies. Over her shoulder, she yelled, "C'mon, Georgie!"

One of the regulars at retro events echoed, "Yeah, c'mon, Georgie!" and dragged her into the mêlée.

She grinned at him, her gypsy skirts flying and the ribbons twined in her hair fluttering and felt a huge surge of delight.

This was *so* her scene.

After dinner, Georgie and Layla joined Tammy and Jerry in his giant black monster of an RV, partly meeting for a rundown on Vintage and Retro sales but primarily to just hang out and talk. For a change, Georgie felt quite warm towards her brother. He was actually helping to grow the vintage division—instead of working against it—and had even made an effort to get in character for the retro crowd. That was *huge*.

He eyed her suspiciously. "Why are you looking at me with that weird little grin? What's wrong?"

"I'm not sure if it's really Jerry I'm looking at," she said, "or if all this is a trick to lull me into a false sense of security."

He flashed her a full-wattage Jerry B. Goode grin, the one that the TV cameras loved and that made women swoon. It usually had no effect whatsoever on her, but tonight, with Jerry in his bad-boy Danny Zuko outfit, it had a certain rakish charm.

Take two ibuprofen and lie down for a while, Georgie, she told herself.

"Tams has been at me forever to come and join in," he said. "So I did. What, you think I don't appreciate the effort you girls are putting in?"

Georgie and Layla looked at each other, and Tammy hid a small smile.

Jerry, always quick to pick up on what was not being said, shrugged. "OK, I might have made a wrong move or two in the past. But I fixed it, didn't I?"

Quelling the impulse to point out that his 'wrong moves', such as threatening to move the vintage trailer division to a seedy part of town, were purely based on self-interest, she simply nodded. "You did. And now you're going above and beyond. But now that you've appeared once, the crowd will expect it." Shamelessly, she piled on flattery. "They loved you. They see you and Tammy as a pair. Better block out all the retro rallies in your diary." She sat back and beamed at him.

"Hear, hear!" Tammy raised her glass in a toast and planted a kiss on Jerry's cheek. "The next one we've scheduled is five weeks away. It's a Happy Days theme. How do you feel about Fonzie?"

A slow smile spread across Jerry's face. He put his head on one side while he regarded Tammy, looking sexy and irresistible in her black Sandy spandex and killer red heels. A tiny hint of calculation flashed in his eyes.

Uh oh, thought Georgie. Some kind of trade-off coming up here…

"Sure, babe," he said easily, reaching across to tug on one tousled blonde curl. "Fonzie's an easy move sideways from Danny Zuko. Who are you going to be?"

"Joanie, I guess." She grinned at him and turned sideways to lie back on one of the charcoal and ebony striped armrests, casually plunking her feet across his knees.

Jerry eased off one red shoe and massaged her foot while Tammy heaved out a sigh. "Oh, that feels good. I love these shoes, but my feet are killing me. *Hours* of dancing."

"Find some saddle shoes and go bobbysoxer," Layla said, sticking out a foot to show her practical footwear. "Dance all night and come up laughing."

"But she looks so good in heels," Jerry objected, slipping off the second red shoe and holding it up like a trophy before putting it down and resuming his duties as a masseur. Then he added casually, "Might as well wear them now; she won't be in high heels to talk with the preppers. No dancing at the Apocalypse." He laughed.

And there it is, thought Georgie. She caught the guarded look in Tammy's eye and raised an eyebrow. "To talk to the preppers…?"

"Quid pro quo," Tammy explained, her smile somewhat forced. "Jerry puts in time with vintage if I do the same with preppers."

Georgie waved a hand at all the black spandex. "You never wear anything but retro, Tams. How are *you* going to help sell bug-out vehicles and 'Get Out Of Dodge' packs?"

"Retro might not be quite the look," Jerry allowed, "although survivalists are learning more about traditional farming and crafts. Home-grown food, making do, recycling clothes. But it's Tammy's former life that we're calling on."

From the other side of the RV, reclining in a leather chair, Layla sat up and paid attention. "Tams! You were a *prepper*? No, you *weren't.*"

"Of course I wasn't." Tammy did a little shimmy in her skin-tight Grease outfit, a movement that had Jerry grinning in appreciation. "Do I *look* like one?"

"Not right now," Georgie said, "but remember, we've seen you go incognito. You could play anyone."

"Preppers don't have a 'look', anyway." Jerry warmed to his theme. "They have a lifestyle. They don't all dress like commandos, but they're prepared for all eventualities. Tams can talk to anyone. Throw in a few guns, and what prepper could resist her?"

Georgie and Layla spoke at the same time. "*Guns?*"

"Jerry," Tammy said warningly, "I told you, no guns."

"You don't have to fire them. Just talk about them as though you know what you're doing."

"And how, exactly, is Tammy supposed to know anything about guns?" Georgie asked.

Jerry looked faintly guilty, as though he had betrayed a confidence. "Uh…well…you tell them, babe."

Tammy rolled her eyes and hitched herself up, kicking free of Jerry's grip. She drew up her knees and wrapped her arms around them, a tiny crease in her forehead. "I know guns, all right?" she said reluctantly. "My aunt is a crack shot, and she taught me. And I've done…advanced training." She looked away as she said it, clearly telegraphing: *don't go there.*

"So Tams and I came to an agreement." Jerry grinned at them all happily. "I play Danny Zuko and make nice at the retro meets. I help to expand the division. In return, she talks guns and survival in the wild with preppers."

"I'm not wearing camo gear." Tammy pointed a finger at him with a clear warning in her blue eyes.

"Wouldn't dream of asking you to, honey. Just forget the swing skirt and bobby sox, OK?"

While listening to their exchange, Georgie had been watching their body language.

Tammy was not comfortable with this.

Jerry, on the other hand, was not only comfortable but was hiding something. The one thing he couldn't control was that telltale twitch in his jaw, the sure signal, over their years growing up together, that her brother was up to no good.

She was determined to find out what was going on.

CHAPTER 3

A Premonition

The following day Georgie and Layla waved as Tammy pulled away with her cherry red and white trailer in tow. A cheerful little loop of scarlet flags strung along the truck fluttered in the breeze.

She slowed and stuck her head out of the window as she passed by, her Sandy curls peeking out from under a cherry-sprigged bandana. "See you back at Elkhart!"

Georgie nodded. "Three days!"

Jerry rolled along behind her in his monster black and gold RV, casting a shadow over them as he passed. Unlike Tammy, he had ditched the retro look in favor of cargo pants and a t-shirt with the Johnny B. Goode logo. "Bye, girls!" He pointed a finger at Georgie and grinned annoyingly. "Keep those sales targets up, now!"

Georgie choked back an unladylike reply and merely smiled coolly, which simply earned her a laugh. Her brother had always liked pressing her buttons.

He moved on, and she watched him follow Tammy's trailer out of the campground and up the road, staring after them until they were out of sight, frowning.

Disquiet curled within her.

Layla touched her arm. "What's up?"

Georgie turned to meet her friend's concerned gaze. "I don't know. I just feel that something's… off. Like I should run after Tammy and tell her to be careful." She shook her head. "But careful of what? It's just a feeling."

By now, Layla knew that if Georgie said she had a bad feeling about something, it was time to take notice. "Time to talk to the crystal ball?" she suggested tentatively.

Georgie's experiences with the crystal ball over the past few days didn't give her much hope, but it was worth a go. Anything to quell this queasy feeling of almost-dread in her gut.

"I'll give it a shot. You keep packing up; I'll come over when I'm done."

All around them, people were hitching up retro trailers, many of them to vintage cars. It was a casual process, with plenty of catch-up chats going on at the same time. As usual, everyone was reluctant to leave.

Georgie, dressed in Boho pants and a drawstring blouse, ran up the steps of her trailer and closed the door against the noise of departure. She needed to concentrate.

The crystal ball rested on its usual shelf, covered with Rosa's old velvet cloth. "*Please*," Georgie murmured as she moved it to the table and slid off the covering. "I need *something*…"

She rested her hands on the globe and closed her eyes, thinking of Tammy and Jerry heading off on the road to Elkhart. Were they going to be involved in an accident?

No, she thought, that wasn't it. They were going to reach Elkhart safely, but what was in store for them after that?

Under her fingertips, the crystal ball stayed firm and cool. Georgie concentrated harder, but her thoughts kept intruding, skittering around in her mind like nervous mice. Tammy, Jerry, Tammy, Jerry… they were her *family; she had* to see what was coming.

No matter how hard she tried, she got nothing.

Nothing at all.

Georgie opened her eyes and looked bleakly at the crystal ball, knowing what she'd see. Clear, cold crystal gleaming in the bright morning light filtering through the stained glass windows. There was none of the growing warmth that she'd come to expect; no soft white mist that allowed messages through.

If only Scott were here. Her mind filled with the image of his open, friendly face and smiling eyes, the color of whisky in sunlight. He'd been gone for three weeks now after answering a call for help from a former work buddy in the Cherokee National Forest in Tennessee. Thank goodness he was getting close to the end of his relief stint. She hadn't realized how much she would miss his steady presence in her life until he was gone.

She smiled, remembering his calm assertion at the rally back in California. *We're going to get married one day, but don't worry about it now.*

Married to Scott… She had no idea how that would work once his visa expired and he had to return to Australia. She was committed to the vintage trailer division of her father's RV Empire back here. She could foresee lots of problems with sorting that one out.

But right now, he *wasn't* here, and she still had

the problem of what was going to happen to Tammy.

She sighed and picked up Rosa's velvet cloth to cover the crystal ball again.

They'd be back in Elkhart in a few days. By then, her great-grandmother would be climbing the walls with her enforced inactivity, getting crankier by the minute and making her grandson Johnny's life a misery. She would probably welcome a visit—and maybe Georgie could find out what was going on with her crystal ball.

A gypsy fortune-teller whose crystal ball was malfunctioning. What a joke.

Tea Leaves

Three days later, Georgie was making tea in Rosa's compact kitchen and already, after ten minutes, wishing she were anywhere else. The moment she arrived, her great-grandmother had launched into an indignant account of how people were treating her like a baby, and she didn't need coddling, and they just didn't breed people tough anymore. In her comfortable chair by the window, with her sprained ankle up on an ottoman, she was still venting. Her unfortunate day nurse, overwhelmingly grateful to be told to go and take an hour off away from Rosa's interminable grumbles, had just scurried out of the door.

"As though I need a nurse," Rosa griped. "A *nurse*. Waste of good money. Your father knows I'm capable of looking after myself."

"Of course you are," Georgie agreed, carrying in a tray with two teapots and cups and the carrot cake that Rosa favored. "When you don't have a sprained ankle. But right now, you need a bit of help. Remember what the doctor said: the last thing you need is to fall and break a hip."

Rosa wasn't feeling receptive to common sense. She waved that away with a disgusted 'Pah!" and accepted a cup of tea. "Did you warm the pot first? And let it steep?"

"Yes, I know you like it strong." Georgie put a plate with a slice of cake on the side table next to Rosa, and picked up the second teapot, and poured her own tea, inhaling the delicate fragrance of Earl Grey.

Rosa eyed the second teapot with disfavor. "When did you start drinking that perfumed muck?"

"Layla converted me." Georgie grinned. "You haven't met Layla yet. She's on our road team for retro trailers." She sat in the chair opposite Rosa and sipped, closing her eyes in appreciation. "Lovely. How's yours?"

Rosa tried hers. "It's good enough, I suppose."

"You must be pretty bored, sitting here all day. Dad tells me you're supposed to be confined to bed. I can imagine how well that suggestion went down."

"I don't know why I can't go to the RV yard. At least there's always something happening there."

"Trucks and RVs are moving around all the time; while you're indisposed, you can't get out of the way quickly."

"I could sit in the showroom or the waiting room."

There was no way Georgie was going to win this one. Rosa was grumpy and still suffering some pain, and she was going to let the world know it.

Time to change the subject.

"The crystal ball," she said. "It's not working for me."

"I was wondering when we'd get to that."

Georgie put her head on the side and sent Rosa a quizzical glance. "You already knew?"

"Not for sure, but it's been harder for me to get through and know what you're up to." Rosa shrugged. "It was always going to happen."

Georgie felt her shoulders relax as a surge of relief swept through her. "So it's not just me? It happened to you too?"

"Happens to pretty much anyone who uses a crystal ball," Rosa said. "Sometimes I sit back and picture the Gods sitting up there in the clouds some-where, having a great old laugh at our expense.

Lying around and eating grapes and drinking mead and talking about how humans always expect to have their questions answered." Without thinking, she went to move her foot away from the ottoman, then winced and wriggled in discomfort. "Damned ankle. We don't appreciate being mobile until we're not."

Georgie sat forward. "Can I get you another cushion for your leg?"

"No, then it's too high. Don't worry about it," Rosa snapped. She was silent for a moment and then said abruptly, "Sorry. I'm a pain in the rear end, I know."

In a flash, Georgie went from being irritated by her to feeling guilty. She could only imagine what it must be like to be ninety-three—or was it ninety-four?—and confined to a chair with a sprained ankle. Difficult at any age, but much more challenging when you were older.

"Don't give it a thought," she said. "I don't like having to sit still for long myself. Which makes things tricky when I'm spending a good chunk of each morning sitting at a table with a crystal ball."

"Word is that you're not charging for a reading?" Rosa watched her, sipping slowly at her tea.

"That's right. If they don't pay, they can't criticize."

Then she and Rosa both said at the same time, "But they still do," and both laughed.

"I don't need the money," Georgie pointed out. "Not with my commissions, and with Dad's business, I'm set for the future. I just put out the sign so anyone who needs me can find me."

Rosa's eyes were keen as she studied Georgie's face. "And how's that working out? People finding you?"

Georgie gave her a quick overview of the kind of people who came to her, as well as a run-through of the three cases she had solved so far. Her account of Nick, the teenager with the spy video pen who was determined to hand her over to the cops, saw Rosa's leathery, wrinkled face break out in a broad grin. "I remember that kid," she said. "Passed on a message for him, didn't I?"

"Yes, you did," Georgie said with some asperity, remembering that day with the crystal ball when Rosa's voice had sounded in her ear. "You told me that his mother wanted him to feed his dog. That was *really* useful in solving the case."

Rosa winked. "Got to let you do your own thing."

Thinking about the crystal ball brought Georgie back to the primary purpose of her visit. "Anyway, back to the crystal ball. How long will I have to wait until it…readjusts itself, or whatever it has to do? The thing is…" She hesitated, not sure of whether she should be worrying Rosa.

"Go on," her great-grandmother commanded. "Spit it out."

"I think Tammy is headed for trouble," Georgie said in a rush. "And Jerry, too—but I'm not so concerned about him; he can look after himself." She set her cup down and leaned forward, her hands linked on her lap while she stared at Rosa. "Something's going to happen, Grandma Rosa, and right now, I can't see what it is. I haven't even warned them yet, because I don't know what to tell them. I *need* the crystal ball working again. Unless—" She bit her lip. "Unless you could try?"

Rosa had gone very still. "You say you see something coming?"

"Kind of. I can't *see* anything. But I *know* it. I do. I just don't know what."

Opposite her, Rosa stared down at the cup and said quietly, "I haven't felt a thing. Nothing."

Georgie hid her alarm. *Rosa* couldn't see anything, either? "Well, you've been sick. You were knocked out for a few minutes, Dad said, and you've had headaches."

"Doesn't matter. The Sight gets past all that."

Rosa suddenly looked shrunken and old. "I thought I'd have it until death."

"Do you want to try the crystal ball?"

"No, not if it's not working for you." She drained the rest of her tea and stared into the cup. Her eyes narrowed, and she lost focus, as though she was staring right through the cup to the floor and down to the center of the earth. Then she tilted the cup and turned it around a few times before glancing up at Georgie. "Come here."

"I'd forgotten that you read tea leaves as well as the crystal ball. And cards." Georgie leaped to her feet and went across to look over Rosa's shoulder. The tea leaves clumped in a few places, and she saw something that might have been a horse's head, or maybe a bucket?

She sighed. "Means nothing to me."

"That's because you're trying to make them into any symbols that make sense to you. Just stare at them, and let your mind go blank."

"It's been blank for days," Georgie muttered unhappily but did as Rosa asked. She stared until the tea leaves blurred together and then, crazily, began to take on some meaning.

Leaves. Not tea leaves, but leaves, generally, thick and clustered. Branches, trees.

A forest?

Yes, a forest. Some wilderness area.

She blinked, and the tea leaves came back into focus again, but somehow she could see that yes, that odd clump there somehow meant…out in the wild.

"A forest," she said. "Wait." She did the same thing again, and from the blur came an impression of shadowy figures. It was so strange: she couldn't picture them, but she *could* sense what was going on. The *meaning* came through.

"People, in the forest." As she said it, pain lanced into her forehead. "Ow."

Rosa's free hand reached back and clamped on her forearm. "You feel pain?"

"A sudden headache."

"Not anywhere else? Chest, legs, anywhere?"

"No. Why?"

"Sometimes, it can mean an injury in a particular part of the body. A headache is usually just tied to the difficulty of getting a message. Was for me, anyway."

The pain abruptly lessened and became a dull ache, and Georgie sighed with relief. "What about you? Are you getting anything?"

"No." The desolation in Rosa's voice was heartbreaking. "Not a thing."

So it's down to me, Georgie thought. *I'm right,*

though: something's going to happen to Tammy, or Jerry, or both.

Once more, she tried opening her mind to the meaning hidden in the tea leaves, but the more she tried to concentrate, the more her headache throbbed.

"I can't do any more." Reaching down to take the cup from Rosa, she saw her great-grandmother's hand trembling. She squeezed the old woman's shoulder and returned to her chair, seeing her fear reflected in Rosa's eyes.

"What should we do?" she asked.

"Tell them what you've seen," said Rosa. "Do it now. Danger in a forested area, from unknown people. It's better than nothing."

Georgie swallowed hard and told her: "Jerry was going to get Tammy to talk to his Preppers. Something about guns."

"Oh my Lord. Go. Go now."

"But your nurse…"

"I won't move until she gets back. Go on, don't dilly dally!"

Georgie gave her great-grandmother a hug and a kiss, snatched up her bag with the useless crystal ball, and left, her heart thumping erratically.

CHAPTER 5

The Barbarian

E arlier that morning, bumping his way along a corrugated track in northern Kentucky, Jerry had been feeling particularly happy and pleased with the world. As he drove, he whistled a prepper's song that one of his cashed-up survivalist customers had taught him. The words were set to the tune of John Denver's "Thank God I'm a Country Boy", which was nice and easy to remember. The re-vamped chorus had nothing about country boys but ran along the lines of 'thank God I'm a prepper now', while the rest of the song had bits and pieces about a world under attack and putting the pedal to the metal. It kind of appealed to Jerry. Every so often, he broke off whistling to sing the parts that he could remember while occasionally glancing at the GPS.

They'd be waiting for him about twenty miles from the turnoff, Vincent had told him, and he'd done nigh on eighteen miles now, so he'd have to be getting close.

The truck crashed down into another pothole, which didn't concern him in the slightest. He was in the Jerry B. Goode BugOut Barbarian—"Barbie" for short—the best prepper vehicle they'd produced yet, and Vincent was about to put it through its paces and then order his own if he was satisfied.

Like there was anyone who tried it who *wasn't* satisfied. You couldn't stop this baby.

Hello, quarter of a million dollars!

Jerry took his hand off the wheel for a moment to reach over and pat himself on the back, and then rounded a bend to find a lean, fit boss-man type and another huge guy who must be the hired gorilla waiting by the side of the road, leaning on a 4WD. It was parked next to the entry point of an over-grown track.

Jerry slowed and stuck his head out of the window. "You'd be Vincent?"

"I would." The guy moved his lips in a move-ment that might have been a smile and moved forward to pat the rugged side of BugOut Barbie. "Lookin' good there, Jer. Can't wait to try this one out." He moved closer, his expression wary and his dark eyes sharp. "You sure nobody followed you here?"

"Certain," Jerry assured him. Man, these guys were paranoid. Always afraid that someone would find out about their bug-out vehicles and burrows in the ground—or a fortress on some hill with its back to a rugged rock wall.

"You didn't put the coordinates on a computer where people can find them, nothin' like that?"

"The only coordinates are in here," Jerry assured him, tapping on the GPS screen. He grinned. "I ate the piece of paper I jotted them down on."

Vincent looked at him without smiling. "You can laugh, but when things go to hell, you'll be knocking on my door like everyone else."

"I know, I know. Just having a bit of fun with you, man." Jerry reached out and knocked knuckles with him. "We take security seriously at the RV Empire."

"Hackers can get in anywhere."

"Your details are not on our computers, right? Not on my phone, not written down anywhere. Nobody's going to find you. Nobody that you don't want to, anyway."

"Okay." Vincent unbent a little. "Follow us, then."

Jerry watched him swing into his truck with the other guy—who looked just as suspicious— and rolled his eyes.

A quarter of a million, he reminded himself. It wasn't money anyone would invest lightly. You had to expect a bit of paranoia from guys who were willing to spend this kind of money.

He put Barbie into gear and swung past a couple of scraggy bushes to follow them.

He couldn't wait to see their bunker.

Back at the vintage trailer division of the RV Empire, Tammy stood back and surveyed the newest retro-style trailer. For two guys who didn't give a rat's about vintage, Jerry and his dad had nailed their customer base. They'd picked four basic shapes—one modeled on the Airstream, another on the Shasta, and a couple of others in between—and offered a range of embellishments to give any mock-vintage trailer the exact look the customer wanted. Any color, decals, rounded windows, square windows…it was all there for the asking.

The new trailer was pink and white, shaped like a lozenge, and looked good enough to eat. Inside were ruffled curtains with a polka dot trim and delicate china cups in fairy floss pink and pale green. Irresistible. Tammy nodded in satisfaction, tweaked the polka dot cloth on the round table outside it, and thought about whether a hint of jet black here and there might add some vibrancy to the mood.

"Hey Tams," came a voice behind her. "It's gorgeous. Did you do the interior?"

"Georgie, hi." Tammy turned and gave her a quick hug. "I had a hand in it. How's Rosa?"

"Cranky, in pain, and frustrated at being confined to barracks. Pretty much what you'd expect… yet I think she was happy to see me."

Tammy looked at her keenly, noting the smile. "You sound surprised."

"Well, Rosa and I have always had an up-and-down relationship. It's changing, I think, because of the crystal ball and the Sight thing." Her forehead creased. "Tams…about that…"

Tammy had known Georgie long enough to recognize that particular inflection in her voice. Her friend had something to say and was unsure of how it would be received. She sat in one of the black wrought iron chairs at the small table and indicated the other one. "What's up?"

Georgie sat in the second chair, sitting forward uncomfortably, her hands clenched in her lap. Her eyes held Tammy's.

"Tams, I'm going to just come out and say it. I think something's going to happen to either you or Jerry. Or both. I can't tell you what—you know what trouble I've been having with the crystal ball. But I told Rosa, and she did a tea leaf reading—or rather, I did—and I didn't pick up much, but the *feeling* is still there." There was a small silence, and then she added in a small voice, "I know it's not much, and it's as vague as all hell, but that's all I've got. So all I can say is, be *careful.* Please."

Tammy felt her heart lurch. Georgie wouldn't be here telling her this if she wasn't anxious.

"You didn't see anything?"

"Nothing specific. I saw leaves, trees, like a forest or a wilderness area. And a few shadowy people." Georgie closed her eyes for a moment, and Tammy could see that she was trying to recall it. "I didn't *see* the people, I sensed them. I haven't read tea leaves before, so I didn't really know what I was doing."

Tammy just sat there for a moment, caught by surprise. "I don't know what to say. More important, I don't know what to *do.* "

"Me neither," said Georgie with a hollow laugh. "Just be careful. That's all I can say. And tell Jerry. I'm not sure what his reaction will be; he's always treated Rosa's crystal ball as a bit of a joke—

window dressing for the gypsy trailer. I don't know if he believes that it works."

Tammy thought back to how their little group had used the crystal ball's predictions back in Santa Monica and before that in Dayton. "I told him about the cases you've solved... like the last one with Nick and how we put things together from your crystal ball readings." She added reluctantly, "Even so, I don't know how seriously he takes it. I think he thought I was exaggerating."

Well, she thought, Jerry could darn well take it seriously *now*; she would see to that. It was more than time he gave his sister the credit she deserved.

She stood up, leaned over, and patted Georgie on the shoulder. "I'll go find Jerry; he's due back in Dumpsville about now with that new bug-out vehi-cle... what did they call it? The Barbarian?" She rolled her eyes. "*Barbarian.* Men! Let's meet up in an hour, right? Are you staying at your Dad's house?"

"Yes. But can we make it an hour later? I heard from Scott this afternoon. He's heading back from Cherokee Park. If we wait, and I grab Layla, we can all meet up for a council of war."

"Perfect," Tammy said. "The Crystal Ball Inves-tigation team back together again...only with Jerry there too." She sent Georgie a rueful look. "I'm not sure how the team will feel about *that.*"

"Whatever it is that's coming, Jerry's in it up to his neck," Georgie assured her, looking marginally happier to be taking some action.

"Done. I'll find someone to pack all of this away for the night and go find Jerry."

Georgie nodded. "I'll locate Dad, give him an update on Rosa, and catch you later."

Tammy watched her make her way toward the main building, an unlikely-looking gypsy fortune teller in blue jeans and an asymmetric navy t-shirt. It was a reminder that although she might wear flowing gypsy skirts and shawls a lot of the time, just as Tammy herself usually dressed in vintage clothes, real life wasn't a dress-up party.

There were real threats to happiness out there.

CHAPTER 6

The Team Gathers

Several hours later, when she answered the chimes to the front door of her father's house, one look at Tammy's face told Georgie that her warning had come too late. Her heart sank.

"He's missing, Georgie." Tammy was trying to sound calm, but Georgie could hear the strain in her voice. "Nobody has seen him since yesterday. Except me, but I was still half asleep when he left this morning."

"Wait, save it for the others, so you don't have to tell it twice." Georgie gave her a quick hug, then led the way to the media room with its soft couches. "Dad and Angela are out, thank goodness, so we can talk this through without him going off the deep end."

Layla and Scott were waiting, and their expressions changed when they saw Tammy's expression. Layla immediately bounced to her feet and took her arm. "Come sit by me. No Jerry?"

"No." Tammy took a seat and crossed her arms tightly over her chest. She was still wearing her pink swing skirt with the musical notes on it in black and the neat little shirt that went with it. With her high bouncy ponytail, she looked like a high school kid sitting and waiting for the Principal. She swallowed a couple of times.

Scott passed Tammy the wine that he had poured when Georgie answered the door and gave her shoulder a supportive squeeze.

"Thanks, Scott." She sat there holding it, staring into the glass, and then seemed to gather herself. Her chin came up, and she took a deep breath. "Let me tell you what I've been able to find out. First, nobody at the BugOut Base has seen Jerry since yesterday afternoon at around 3 o'clock. He was out last night at some local government dinner, and I was in bed when he got home. This morning he left at around five—said he had a long round trip to make, but he'd be back late after-noon, dinner time at the latest." She paused and toyed with the stem of her glass. "I didn't ask where he was going; he's always heading off *somewhere*."

"And you hadn't heard anything from him when I saw you this afternoon?"

"No, there was no reason. I was busy setting up the new trailer, and he always calls when he can." Her voice hitched a little on the 'when he can'. "So after I saw you, I went straight out to the BugOut Base to talk to the guys. They were all still there, doing overtime to fill the orders. Jerry had checked out in Barbie but left no details of where he was going." She sighed. "Anybody else would risk being fired if they did that, but because Jerry's the boss… well, anyway, he didn't tell them."

Georgie looked at her blankly. "Barbie?"

"The newest bug-out vehicle. Equipped with everything for the day everything goes ballistic. That thing I was talking about earlier. They called it the BoV Barbarian, Barbie for short."

"What about satellite tracking?" asked Scott.

"I thought of that right away. I got Danny to check. The last coordinates were in Kentucky."

"*Kentucky?*" Layla said. "What's he doing there?"

"He goes all over to visit preppers." Tammy nibbled on a fingernail, her forehead creased. "If it's a long way, he'll fly, but if he's demonstrating a bug-out vehicle, he'll drive it there. The guys all assumed that's what he did today."

Georgie had picked up a lot about the preppers

scene from Jerry, and had consulted with him on fabrics and design for the interior of the early bug-out vehicles. She'd got to know the layout and fittings well. "He's got an onboard satellite phone. Can you reach him on that?"

"It's out of action, just like his phone. And nobody knows who he was meeting today." Tammy picked up her phone from the table and tapped a few buttons before pointing at the screen. "I got Danny to email a list of all the people Jerry's been talking with in the past few weeks and their contact details—but there's no guarantee that the person he was meeting is there. It could be somebody from months back."

"What about the CB radio?"

"The vehicle has a combo MURS/FR. We could probably raise someone down that way to try to contact him on it, but—" Tammy stopped for a fraction of a second, then pushed on, "but Jerry has to be able to get to it to use it."

"I hate to state the obvious," Layla said, "but do we want to call in the police?"

"Last resort," Tammy said. "His prepper busi-ness will collapse if the police are allowed access to private information. The customers are all para-noid." She immediately corrected herself. "No, actually they're not; I've met a lot of nice people who just want to give themselves a chance of survival if things go bad. But there are a *lot* who are paranoid."

Georgie's phone beeped, and they all froze.

She picked it up from the side table, glanced at the screen, and shook her head. "Not him. Hang on." She swiped at it and put it on speaker. "Hi, Rosa."

Her great-grandmother said without preamble, "Young Jerry's already in trouble, isn't he?"

They all knew it, but hearing Rosa's ancient voice saying it baldly over the phone made it so much more real. Tammy's eyes immediately grew bright, and she bit her bottom lip.

"Yes, we think he might be," Georgie said, deliberately keeping her voice steady. Tammy didn't need anyone breaking down. "He's gone missing. We're all at Dad's—me, Tammy, Scott, and Layla— trying to work out what to do next." Georgie asked the question in everybody's mind. "How did *you* know?"

"I just know. The boy's my blood."

"Do you know where he is?"

"Only that it's some distance from here. It's no good looking around Elkhart; you won't find him."

"We think he's in Kentucky—or that's as far as the vehicle got, anyway. Can you wait a second?"

Georgie looked at Tammy. "What time was the last reading on the satellite tracker?"

"Danny's on it…wait." Tammy scrolled through her messages again. "Around 11 am. He says whoever they are, they know what they're doing. An alert is supposed to come through if a tracker is tampered with, and we should also be able to immobilize the vehicle from the base." She looked up. "Didn't happen."

"It's probably not where it was the last time the tracker registered it, then. They'll have moved on."

Georgie held up a hand and returned to Rosa. "Did you catch that?"

"Yes." Rosa's crack of laughter held no humor whatsoever. "Young pup swears by his new-fangled devices. Wonder what he says now." Then her voice softened marginally. "Don't you fret, Tammy girl. We don't need satellite trackers."

Maybe, gypsies whose crystal balls *work* don't need trackers, Georgie thought. "Do you want one of us to pick you up, Rosa? Bring you here? You could stay here with us tonight."

"Not tonight. You put your heads together and come up with a plan, and I'll contact you when I know anything." Her voice grew louder. "Tammy?"

Tammy, lost in thought, jerked upright. "Yes, I'm here."

"You'll be going after him with the others," Rosa said in a tone that brooked no argument. "Jerry has certain equipment over there at that BugOut place. Be prepared to use it; I know you know how."

Stunned, Georgie gazed at the phone. This was *Rosa?* She was obviously a lot savvier with what was going on around the RV Empire than any of them gave her credit for. She glanced across at Tammy, who had a strange look on her face. Her eyes met Georgie's and narrowed, and then she gave a short, sharp nod.

Georgie would have to follow up on that later. Was Rosa talking about guns? There couldn't be any over at the BugOut Base, surely; they didn't have a license to sell firearms. She put that thought aside. "Rosa, you've seen something about us going after him? Tell us."

"That's it. I see you following his trail. You get that crystal ball out and use any other means—tea leaves, cards, water scrying for all I care—to find your brother. Young Scott, you look at the cards too and call your mother. You know wilderness areas, so be prepared. Layla, you've got a good head on your shoulders, so get thinking."

Rosa was on the warpath; nobody was messing with *her* family.

"OK," Georgie said. "What about Dad?"

"You'll have to tell him." A hint of slyness entered her great-grandmother's voice. "But wait until you're about to leave. He'll try to stop you; you're his baby girl."

"All right. I'm ending the call now, but I'll keep you informed. Anything else you want to tell us?"

"Just find my great-grandson. There's a lot of good in the boy, underneath those conniving ways."

With that, Rosa was gone, without waiting for Georgie to cut the connection.

CHAPTER 7

Prepped and Ready

J erry had to concede that he was in a bit of a fix.

If there was one thing that he prided himself on, it was his ability to adapt to circumstances. He was a chameleon, gifted at reading a situation and swiftly figuring out a way to turn it to his advantage. Or sometimes, how to get himself out of trouble. When you grew up with an eye to the main chance, you were going to run into trouble sometimes.

But this—*this* was like no other situation he'd ever found himself in before, and he wasn't having much luck at talking his way out of it. He'd tried anger, indignation, threats, promises, half-truths, and bribery, but this Vincent guy just looked at him with dull eyes and said, "We want locations, Mr. Goode, and we're going to get them."

Locations, as in 'give up the bug-out bunkers'—or houses, or fortresses, or whatever the heck people had come up with to give themselves a hidey-hole for the apocalypse. They knew, Vincent said, that Jerry had names and GPS locations. Hacking into the RV Empire computer had revealed nothing, so he obviously kept them somewhere else, and they would like to know where; thank you.

His beloved new bug-out vehicle was already gone; Barbie, it seemed, was on its way to the prepper version of a chop shop. He was a little concerned that he, Jerry B. Goode, could well be on his way to a human chop shop. The thought didn't thrill him.

He touched his head where they'd used a rifle butt to encourage him to be cooperative and closed his eyes against the bolt of pain when he felt the gash. His fingers came away sticky with blood.

"Just a warning," Vincent had said without emotion. "So you know not to mess us about. The locations, if you please. Or we'll be forced to return and pick up that cutesy little girl of yours, see what *she* knows."

It took Jerry a moment to realize that they meant Tammy, and his heart went cold.

Tammy in the hands of this lot?

After telling him to think it over, they left, had now been gone for some time.

He slumped against the wall, fighting a headache, and looked around him for the tenth time in as many minutes. Dark had fallen a good few hours before, and the thin white light from the moon that filtered in through the small barred window high above him didn't illuminate much.

His prison appeared to be some kind of shipping container. Apart from the tiny window, the walls and floor were solid metal. It was equipped, he remembered, with a standard shipping container bolt *and* chains with links as thick as his thumb; impossible to breach.

Cold seeped in through the sides of the container, and there was a light breeze blowing rain through the window.

Shivering, he got up and moved to sit against a side wall.

Now he could understand why preppers were always going on about self-protection and guarding against gangs that wanted to take what was yours. There were a dozen nifty things back at the BoV Base that would have been handy to have in his pockets or his shoe, but he had nothing.

Nada.

Zilch.

But if he *had* hidden something, they'd have found it anyway. They'd taken his watch, his shoes, and everything he had in his pockets, including his phone.

There were lots of photos of Tammy on his phone. Tammy in her vintage outfits, Tammy hamming it up on stage…Tammy dressed in her Sandy outfit from Grease, all allure and tumbling blonde curls.

He drew in a long, slow breath, pushed aside the image of these guys looking at Tammy while they thought of ways to use her as leverage, and tried to organize his thoughts.

No one back at base was going to locate him through the satellite tracker. This lot had disabled that somehow, before trussing him up with cable ties and tossing him in the back before they drove Barbie away. As near as he could judge, they'd been on the road for a couple of hours before they arrived at their destination-maybe more, maybe less. It wasn't easy to judge when you were being tumbled around like a bag of laundry in the back of a truck, wincing at every corrugation.

Two hours, and who knew which direction. He could still be in Kentucky or any of the states surrounding it.

No matter how many times he went through everything, he came up with the same bleak thought: if they were going to find him, it wouldn't be through satellite trackers or phone triangulation or blind luck. It was going to be through his creaky old great-grandmother Rosa or his sister Georgie.

His fate was in the hands of a couple of gypsy fortune-tellers.

Jerry shook his head and then immediately regretted it as pain lanced through him. He slumped against the wall and tried to sleep while he waited for Vincent and his sidekick to come back.

Nearly three hundred miles away, Georgie swung herself into the passenger seat of a rugged all-terrain vehicle from the BugOut Base, slammed the door, and lowered the window to talk to her father. "I guess we're as prepared as we're going to be."

"Tell me what you're doing, every step of the way." His voice was harsh with worry. "I'm giving you 48 hours before I go to the police.

"We'll be fine." As soon as she said it, she realized it was a stupid thing to say. They had no idea what was in store.

"I want you and Jerry both back alive. I

do *not* want to be going to Kentucky to retrieve a couple of bodies."

"You won't be doing that." Georgie took the hand that he put through the window and kissed it. "I can't tell you not to worry, but I can ask you to trust us."

"I don't believe I'm agreeing to this," he said. "You don't even have a plan. Just 'go to Kentucky'."

"Dad," said Georgie softly, "It's not just 'go to Kentucky'. We're going to the spot where he sent the last known GPS coordinates. I'm sure I'll pick up something there." Actually, she wasn't at all sure, but it was the best they had right now. "Go and sit with Rosa. She's got some kind of link to Jerry. We don't know what, but she'll need you there."

He grunted and stepped back. "Go on, then."

Angela, her forehead wrinkled with concern, put her arm around him. "Come on, Johnny. We'll pick up your grandmother first thing in the morning and take her back to our place. It's where she should have been after that accident anyway."

Sitting at the wheel of the truck beside Georgie, Scott was having the last conversation out of the driver's window with the overseer, Danny, going over their plans. He and another of their workers, Juan, hadn't hesitated to stay back until the early hours of the morning to help them prepare for the trip.

"I've heard back from a couple of the Kentucky preppers," Danny was saying. "I'm limiting contact to those we can trust. They'll be using radio contact, and I've given them your phone number." He jerked a thumb over his shoulder at a slight, dark-haired man in his twenties. "Juan here is still checking the computer for more names, but we keep limited contact details there. The trouble is, Jerry kept a lot of it in his head."

Georgie leaned across Scott. "What about on his phone?"

"Jerry only put in numbers if they told him it was a throwaway."

She nodded despondently and clipped on her seat belt. It seemed that Jerry had been too careful: nobody had any way of knowing who the crucial contacts were.

"Thanks for all your help, guys. Better go home and get some sleep." Scott sketched a farewell salute to Danny and Juan and started the engine.

"Nah, we'll stay and keep digging," Danny said. "Might find something else, and we're here if you need us. We can sleep when this is over."

As they pulled away, Georgie blew her father and Angela a final kiss and twisted in her seat to watch them recede into the distance, standing outside the BoV Base bathed in yellow security lights.

"This is going to be bad for them," she said. "All of us heading off, not knowing what's happened to Jerry." She glanced around at Tammy and Layla in the seats behind her. "Do you guys want to talk about plans or try to grab some sleep?"

"Do you honestly think we'd be able to sleep?" Tammy sounded tired but determined. She'd moved past shock and denial to simmering anger, furious both at the preppers who'd taken Jerry and at Jerry himself for letting it happen.

"No," Georgie admitted, "but I thought I'd ask. Can we talk strategy then?"

Scott turned on to the highway and increased the speed. "One," he said, "Head for Barbie's last known location, which means somewhere in Bedford county. Two, keep communications open for Danny." He tossed a question over his shoulder to Tammy. "Got those contact details handy?"

"He gave me eleven names." Tammy leaned forward. "I know you've already looked at them, Georgie, but see if anything kicks in when I read them out loud." She ran through the list, pronouncing each name clearly and waiting for a beat between each one.

After a minute, Georgie shook her head. "No. Still nothing."

"They might not even be their real names," Layla said.

"They probably aren't. But that doesn't matter," Georgie pointed out. "In our first case, I picked up on Peter Fisher's real name, not the alias he was using. It might not be any of those guys on the list, anyway."

"Let's move on to 'three'," Scott said. "Equipment and strategy. Since we don't know what we'll need, I've packed rope, knives, a space blanket, and basic medical supplies—essentially a field kit. Tammy's got guns, and she and I know how to use them."

"Guns?" Georgie frowned. "You've got to be kidding. They've got guns out at the BoV Base?"

"Let's put it this way," Scott said, "they knew how to access guns."

"How come *you* know how to shoot, Scott?" Layla asked. "I mean, I understand about Tammy, with her family being into hunting and all, but you didn't have that background."

"No, but I have to be able to shoot in the wild, put animals down, that kind of thing." He glanced back at Tammy. "Was Danny able to locate that tranquilizer gun?"

"No. I managed to round up a couple of stun guns, though."

"What else?"

"I've got pepper spray in different size cans, and Danny ran through other things I can use at a pinch —you know, keys as a weapon, that kind of thing."

"OK." Scott was silent for a moment, thinking. "If it comes to having to use a gun to protect yourself, Tams, just do it."

She let out a huff of air. "You think I'd hesitate after this?"

Georgie turned around to look at her. "Tammy, what kind of shot *are* you?"

Tammy said nothing for a moment and then said quietly, "Damned good. Or I used to be. Better than my brothers—which they didn't like."

Georgie decided to leave that alone. There was something dark in Tammy's background; she knew instinctively. She wondered, suddenly, if Jerry sensed that too that there was a lot more to Tammy than the bubbly blonde retro chick that people saw on the surface. She was not only clever but nursing some deep hurt.

Anyway, that was something to explore another day.

Right now, it was all about Jerry.

CHAPTER 8

Following the Trail

They drove steadily through the night, tossing around ideas about where Jerry might be and who might have taken him. Who, and why.

As the miles raced away beneath the wheels and natural tiredness took over, the conversation faded out. Layla and Tammy were both dozing in the back seat – at least, they appeared to be. Georgie was reasonably confident that Tammy wouldn't be able to sleep. Her mind would be racing, thinking about what might happen and picturing the worst.

She glanced across at Scott, his face revealing nothing as he watched the highway in front of him. Scott never seemed to be anything else but calm, but she realized that he kept a lot inside. Every so often, the phone chirped, and they would all sit up and listen as the Bluetooth speaker picked it up.

Danny and Juan back at the base were not making much progress. Regrettably, Jerry had taken client confidentiality a little too seriously.

As Scott terminated yet another call that told them nothing new, Georgie put a hand on his arm. "What are you thinking, Scott? Do you have any ideas?"

"Quite a few. Nothing that's going to get us any closer to knowing where to find him, though."

"Tell me what you're thinking, anyway."

"Yes, please do," came Tammy's voice from the back seat. "I'd rather talk about it than just sit here imagining what might be going on."

"OK then. Jerry's into these prepper vehicles, right? And Jerry being who he is, he's quite likely to have come up with some scheme that's going to take him into dangerous territory." He cast a quick look across at Georgie. "Maybe he's promised something and hasn't been able to follow through. Maybe he has learned something, even if he doesn't know it, that has got someone worried."

Tammy's voice came from behind them. "He's pretty careful with the BoV clients, judging who he can trust and who is batshit crazy. Until I started going out to the Base with him, I had no idea they varied so much—but actually, a good many of them are just like we are. All they want to do is give themselves and their family a chance to survive if everything goes to hell."

Georgie nodded. "Understandable. Look at us right now, racing after Jerry. Family is important."

"Having said that," Tammy went on, "back at the base, I've met a few that scare me. They have this maniacal look in their eyes, and they go on and on about how nobody is going to take what's theirs. Jerry wanted me to talk to them about guns, but I couldn't. Not that kind. "Tammy's voice trembled a little. Although she'd been putting on a brave front, they all knew that she was terrified for Jerry. "I think that's who's got him. But I don't know what they want." She hesitated. "Did you bring your crystal ball?"

"Right here on my lap. Don't give up yet, Tams. We'll find him."

"Don't worry; I'm not. I've *never* been one to give up."

The conversation lapsed again, and Georgie went into a kind of daze, running her fingers over the worn old cloth covering the crystal ball. She hadn't wanted to stow it in a bag or out of sight in the back. She needed it near her, just in case it helped her pick up something about Jerry.

She rested her head on the window, her eyes closing, and the last thing she saw before she dropped off to sleep was Scott's profile, occasionally lit by passing headlights, as they kept eating up the miles on their search for her brother.

The feeling of increasing heat under her palms woke her. It took a moment to re-orient herself and make sense of the hum of the vehicle and the dark cabin of the truck, and then she was abruptly awake.

The crystal ball! With growing anticipation, Georgie unwrapped the velvet enough to slide her fingers underneath, so she was making direct contact with the crystal globe, and then closed her eyes again, letting herself drift.

Don't concentrate too hard, she warned herself. Let it come. Let it come.

The crystal ball grew warmer still under her touch, and she drew in a long slow breath. *At last.*

When an image finally materialized, she was startled. It wasn't an image of Jerry or hard-faced preppers with guns. Nothing about survivalists or Doomsday, and no images of an unfriendly dark forest and strange night noises.

Instead, what drifted into her mind was the image of a somewhat plump, motherly-looking woman with warm grey eyes and wavy salt-and-pepper hair cropped short. She was wearing some kind of…Georgie tried to get a clearer picture. Some sort of football supporter's jersey? It didn't look like any team that she was familiar with. It was a kind of maroon color, a bit like the paint she'd chosen for her trailer. And it had what looked like a dragon's head on it. She consciously tried to relax and just let the image float in her head.

The woman wore jeans and had a big grey dog loping by her side. She seemed to be in a garden, and near her was a tree with bright purple flowers on it.

As she looked at the woman, the woman turned and seemed to look back at her. It was almost as though they were watching each other through a kind of mist. She was trying to say something, but Georgie couldn't get what it was.

Some kind of warning about Jerry? A message about where he was?

Then abruptly, the car phone rang again and broke her concentration. The image dissolved.

"Damn," Georgie said out loud, her eyes snapping open. She ran the images through her mind: the woman, the garden, the tree with purple flowers, the dog. Any of it could be important when they were trying to find where they were holding Jerry.

Listening with half an ear to see who was calling them, she bent down to scrounge in the bag at her feet for her notepad and pen. She had to write this down while the pictures in her mind were still clear.

CHAPTER 9

A Plump Lady

"Hi Mum," Scott said, as Georgie switched on the cabin light to see what she was writing. *Woman, football jersey, grey dog, a tree with purple flowers.*

"Scotty!" The voice on the other end was warm and rich and deep, with a tinge of relief. "Where are you?"

"On the way to Kentucky. Have you got anything for me?" He glanced across at Georgie and said unnecessarily, "It's mum. I asked her to do a spread and see what she could pick up." He turned his attention back to the caller. "Just filling Georgie in."

"Ah, Georgie!" his mother sounded delighted. "Nice to meet you at last. I've been trying to get information about you out of Scotty. But he's not being very cooperative."

Georgie gave a tired grin. It was nice to have something to focus on besides the fear and frustration. "He told me you said we'd meet. Unless there's another Libran in his future."

The voice on the other side laughed. "I'm not sure whether he believed me at the time."

"Why is it," put in Scott, "that people like to talk about me as though I'm not here?"

"I guess this isn't the best time to catch up, Georgie, so we'll take a rain check. Anyway, Scotty…" her voice grew serious. "I'm not sure what you've got yourself into, but there is a lot of darkness around you. You take care."

"I always do, you know that. So what have you got?"

"Georgie, I see your brother near a freshwater source. I'm getting something like a creek or moving water – it's not still, like a lake, but wherever he is has something to do with lakes. I know that sounds contradictory. I can see green fields around; I'm getting the impression that it's an area where there are farms – but this place is overgrown, like a wilderness. Maybe look for a private holding somewhere. That's all I'm able to pick up now, except that I feel he's enclosed. Not in a car. I looked at a map of Kentucky, but no one area is coming to me. My eye wants to go toward the middle of the state, but I could be overthinking this. You know how it is."

"I know all right," Georgie said with feeling.

"I bet you do." There was a sound of wry amusement in the woman's voice. "Anyway, Scotty, I'll keep all of you in mind and do another spread for you soon. If you come up with anything new, let me know so I can add it to the mix."

"Before you go…I did pick up on something," Georgie said. "Just before you phoned. It might mean something if we can track Jerry down. I saw a woman, a bit on the chubby side, hair going grey. Eyes a light color, blue or grey." She stopped, thinking. "She was wearing… well, I don't follow sporting teams, but it might mean something to the others. She's wearing a kind of sports jersey, the same color as my trailer." Then she remembered that Scott's mother hadn't seen her trailer. "A deep maroon. It's got a logo, something that looked like a dragon's head. Maybe that's a Kentucky team?"

"A dragon's head?" Scott glanced at her and then returned his gaze to the road.

"That's what it looked like, but it was all a bit vague. Just an impression."

"Hmmm," said Scott's mother. "Anything else?"

"I saw a dog; I don't know the breed—kind of mottled grey, it looked like. And there was a tree with purple flowers. I'll Google it to see if I can identify it. Possibly it grows in a certain part of Kentucky."

"I have a feeling it's probably a Tibouchina," Scott said, his voice sounding odd. "And the dragon's head you saw… might it be a horse's head?"

"Well, yes, it could be." Georgie frowned, looking at his profile. Was he *laughing?*

"Mum," Scott said, "could you pop out to the garden next to the tibouchina and take a selfie, send it through?"

Georgie stared at him and then suddenly understood, her heart sinking.

Oh no. She *hadn't* just described Scott's mother as being 'on the chubby side'…had she?

She leaned towards the speaker on the dashboard. "Are you wearing some kind of football jersey?"

"Er, yes. I'm a bit of a Broncos fan."

"A *bit*," murmured Scott. "Try maniacal."

"I heard that, Scotty. Well, it's the State of Origin game tonight. What do you expect?" Unable to hide her amusement, she continued, "Don't worry about it, Georgie. Did you pick up anything else, apart from a plump lady in a Broncos jersey?"

"Nothing new." Georgie hid her head in her hands, hearing Layla's muffled chuckles.

Scott intervened. "Thanks for that, mum. You've given us something to work on. I'll stay in touch."

"Bye, darling. Take care. Love you."

"Love you too." He pressed the 'end' button on the steering wheel and grinned at Georgie. "A bit chubby, huh?"

"I did *not* say that. I didn't." She groaned.

Layla said from the back seat, "It's so spooky the way you do that. You saw her clearly enough to identify a football supporter's top? In the garden? *And* you caught it just before the phone rang!"

Georgie heaved a huge sigh. "Yes. It looks like the crystal ball is coming good again. Not much help in finding Jerry, though."

Tammy had been very quiet. Georgie swiveled in her seat to look at her, guilty because they'd been laughing. "Don't worry, Tams. We're getting warmer. We'll get Jerry back, so he can continue to make my life a misery."

"So," Scott said. "Maybe around the middle of Kentucky, farmland district, and near running water. But something to do with lakes. That's a wide area."

"We've got more than we had ten minutes ago," Georgie said. She felt a flash of hope. Surely—*surely* —they would get there before anything terrible happened to Jerry.

Kentucky Rain

Chapter 10

With a gentle rain drifting down on a jewel-green countryside, Kentucky might look like a picture postcard, but the rain was not what they needed right now. They had taken a detour and bumped their way through increasingly rough terrain to the GPS coordinates Vincent had given them, but if Jerry had been there, he had left no trace. Georgie tried doing a crystal ball reading again but got nothing.

Back on the highway, they pulled over to the side of the road to consult the map again.

They cracked the windows just a little to let in some air and compared notes. Scott had a Kentucky map unfolded on his lap and stared at it with a frown while Georgie and Layla consulted their tablet computers.

"If your mother's right, Jerry's somewhere in this area." Georgie sketched a circle with her finger on her iPad screen, encompassing the states around Washington, Marion, Boyle, and Lincoln. "We're looking at maybe eight, nine counties. Even more, if she's a little bit out. That's a sizeable chunk of the country when we don't know where he is."

Tammy hunched forward, peering at the screen over Georgie's shoulder. "Switch to Google Earth. Zoom in, and see if you can see some creeks and streams."

"Not for an area that wide. We could be searching for days." Scott looked up from the map, pinched his nose, and blinked a couple of times. "Danny said he found a thumb drive in the back of a drawer, and he's going to get back if there's any extra information on that. That might help. Meanwhile…" he glanced back the map before folding it roughly, "… since we've got nothing else, let's find out where the dead center of Kentucky is and head for that."

"Good as anything else." Layla had started tapping away at her keyboard as soon as Scott spoke. Any plan was better than none. If Scott's mother said Kentucky's center – fine, the middle of Kentucky it would be.

"Here we go. The geographic center is Marion County. Let's get going."

"We can grab some breakfast and a cup of coffee to go when we get there." Scott glanced up at the gradually lightening sky. "There's sure to be a diner open early along the way. I'll just let Danny know where we're heading."

He hit speed dial, had a brief conversation with Danny, and then yawned. "Ready to go?"

From the back seat, Layla's voice sounded. "Wait, I found something else. We could be on the right track here. Look at this." She passed her tablet through to Georgie. "Just south of Marion, there's this long strip of land – see? They call it the land between two lakes. So we've got two of the things your Mom was talking about, Scott."

"Ye-es." Georgie felt doubtful. She handed the tablet back. "But Scott's mother said to look near running water, not lakes."

"Hang on a minute." Scott drummed his fingers on the steering wheel, his face a study in concentration. "Marion County. Something sticks in my mind about that area between the lakes… wasn't it originally between rivers? Can somebody look that up?"

"For a guy that comes from the other side of the

world, you know a lot about our wilderness areas," Georgie said.

Scott shrugged. "I've been over here almost two years, in and out of training courses with National Parks and Forests—you get to find out a lot about the different state forests."

There was a pause, and then Layla spoke. "You're right, Scott. That land is between artificial lakes—they were originally the Cumberland and Tennessee Rivers. Go to the top of the class."

"They're not likely to be in the actual recreation area," Scott said. "Just down that way somewhere – it'd be their own property, I'd say."

Tammy's phone dinged, and she checked her messages. "Another three names from Danny…he said they might help." She scrolled through her email and then sucked in a breath. "Look at this. A couple is living south of Marion—Jack and Sarah Smith." She glanced up. "I wonder… they've got a farm of some kind." She read out the address. "Worth checking?"

Jack and Sarah Smith. The moment she said their names, Georgie's pulse started to race. She bent down and picked up the crystal ball, resting between her feet.

Layla shoved her tablet through the gap between the seats so Georgie and Scott could see it.

"Look at this. They live right down near that strip of land I was talking about. Between the lakes. Or rivers, depending on how you look at it."

"Jack and Sarah Smith. An alias?" Scott mused. He glanced over at Georgie as she unwrapped the crystal ball. "Georgie? Are you getting something?"

"Yes." She put up a hand in a 'shush' motion. "Give me a minute."

The tension in the truck grew as Georgie closed her eyes and focused on the names. *Jack and Sarah Smith.* Immediately, the crystal ball began to feel warmer. Georgie didn't bother looking at it; she simply let images flicker into existence into her mind.

A couple in their thirties, she'd guess: a big guy in a checked shirt; a woman with dark hair dragged back in a no-nonsense ponytail. Two kids… around elementary school age? Impressions came to her swiftly: the woman at a big wooden table in a kitchen, a couple of kids sitting there with books or something in front of them. A small holding tucked away in the bush.

With all of it came a sense of urgency, *go go go…*

Her eyes snapped open. "Go straight there," she said. "Forget the coffee."

"Oh my God," Tammy said, her voice thick

with emotion. "Is that where he is? Have we found him?"

"I didn't get anything about Jerry. But that doesn't mean he isn't there." She could hear the frustration in her own voice. "Sorry, you know the way it works."

Scott started the engine. "When we get close, we'll make sure we're armed. Keep one of the rifles at your feet, Tams, and we'll take handguns."

The very thought of it made Georgie feel sick; guns, kidnapping, a life-or-death dash to save her brother. This wasn't what she had expected when she hit the road with her gypsy trailer.

Life or death. Those words had come so readily to mind; she did not doubt that they were true. She sat back and watched the road unwinding ahead of them, looking out of the window at the grey sky and the rain on the windscreen.

Hang in there, Jerry, she thought. Just hang in there.

They decided to play it as though they had no idea that Jack and Sarah Smith might secretly be crazy preppers who had Jerry imprisoned in some kind of Doomsday bunker. They would start with a phone call asking for help with radio contact and see where it led.

Tammy had been busy jumping from one preppers forum to another, reading the posts, and had bookmarked some Kentucky prepper blogs and groups. Jack and Sarah Smith had posted several times and had joined in a thread about using radios for contact when communications collapsed. It was logical that someone might approach them for advice. She looked them up in the local phone directory and keyed the number into her cell phone.

They waited until they were ten minutes out from the Smith place before pulling over to get the guns ready, and Tammy hit the green call button. "It's early," she said, glancing at her watch. "But if they've got kids, they'll be up."

Sure enough, the phone was answered almost immediately by a woman's voice. "Hello?"

"Am I speaking with Sarah?" asked Tammy.

"Yes."

"Sarah, my name's Tammy Dyson. I work for the Johnny B. Goode RV Empire. You bought a second-hand 4WD from us about six months ago and had it fitted out with a few options."

"Oh!" The woman's voice warmed, although it held a note of caution. "Yes, of course. Is there something wrong?"

"Nothing wrong with the vehicle," Tammy hastened to assure her, "or the sale. But we have run into a bit of a problem." Her eyes met Georgie's. "You met Jerry, I'm assuming, when you were there?"

"Yes, he was lovely. Very helpful."

"He drove one of our new units down here to Kentucky yesterday morning, and unfortunately, he's now missing. We believe you and Jack know a bit about radios and surveillance, so we were wondering if we could ask for your help?"

"He's *missing*? Like, he's just disappeared?" There was a muttered question in a male voice in the background, and they could hear Sarah giving a quick explanation. She came back on. "You think he came down to see a prepper family here?"

"We don't know whether it's a family or an individual, but the last GPS reading for the truck was in northern Kentucky."

"Northern Kentucky." She sounded puzzled. "But that's miles away. What brought you down here?"

"A possible sighting," Tammy lied. "The thing is, Sarah, we're quite close to you now. Do you think we might pop in and talk?"

"You're *here?*"

"Maybe ten miles from you. But look, if it's too early, that's okay. We can make it later."

"No, no, of course, come now! If Jerry's missing… do you know how to find us?"

"Yes, we have all your contact details from the sale."

"I'll make coffee," Sarah said. "See you soon."

Tammy terminated the call. "Time to roll," she said. "Let's hope we're not jumping straight into trouble."

CHAPTER 11

Preppers

They bumped along the track that led to the Smiths' place, drove through a gate, and pulled up alongside a solid-looking 4WD that bore a Johnny B. Goode RV Empire sticker on its rear bumper. A dog that looked like part Staffy and part who-knew-what barked half-heartedly from near the door and wandered over to sniff at them.

They all piled out into misting rain, watching the dog warily, but he just wagged his tail and submitted to Scott scratching his head. "Not a fierce guard dog then, little guy?" Scott commented before straightening up to survey the house.

Georgie cast a glance at him, but she couldn't see any evidence that he was carrying a gun. Ditto with Tammy, clad in a hunting vest and cargo pants; she had pockets everywhere. With her blonde hair caught up under a cap and no makeup on, she looked ready for a day's hiking. Or hunting. 'Sandy' from Grease had disappeared entirely.

At that moment, the door opened to reveal the real-life version of the woman that fitted the mental picture that Georgie had picked up earlier. Dressed in jeans and a chambray shirt with a loose sweater pulled over the top, she had tanned skin, fine laughter lines around her eyes, and dark brown hair pulled back in a practical ponytail.

"Don't stand around in the rain, come in!" she called, standing back with the door wide open. "I've got coffee…have you been driving all night?"

"Pretty much," Scott said. They gratefully moved in out of the rain, which got heavier as Sarah closed the door.

"You'll be hungry too. Breakfast? Do you have time for eggs and bacon, or do you need to get on with the search?"

Georgie could have kissed her. Coffee, eggs, and bacon sounded like a gift from the gods. "Sarah, that's so kind of you. All of that would be fantastic. We'll be sure to replace your supplies."

"Don't be silly; anything we can do to help."

"Thank you. I'm Georgie. This is Scott, Layla, and Tammy."

They followed Sarah into a good-sized family

living area, with six sturdy chairs around a wooden table. A pixie-like girl of about ten and a solid boy a few years younger sat there with empty cereal plates in front of them, staring at the newcomers with curious eyes.

"These are our kids, Carley and Mason… kids, can you move over to the sofa with your tablets now? Headphones on, please. If you finish your work early, you can choose your own activity later." Efficiently, she shepherded them to an adjacent area and started them on an online learning activity.

"Homeschooling?" Georgie asked when she returned.

"Yes. We made the choice years ago, and it's worked out well. It helped that I was an elementary school teacher before Carley was born." There was a flash of movement to one side, and she glanced over. "Here's Jack, with the radios. Jack, let me introduce you to our guests." She ran through the introductions.

Jack, a tall man in his thirties with steady hazel eyes and a thick crop of greying brown hair, stood in the doorway between the kitchen and a corridor, his arms laden with electronic equipment. He nodded a welcome but didn't smile, his eyes moving from one face to another. "Welcome to our home.

I'm sorry to hear about your problems; I hope we can help."

Sarah exchanged the flicker of a glance with him, and Georgie was instantly on the alert. A lot was going unsaid here. The pair could be posing as harmless citizens that liked an alternate lifestyle and homeschooling on the surface, she thought, while hatching who knew what plans on an entirely different level.

"Take a seat, everyone," Sarah said. "Not the chair at the end; Jack always sits there. I'll get breakfast started while you fill him in. Everyone happy with poached eggs, bacon, and sausage?"

"Thank you." Georgie gestured towards the kitchen counter, where eggs rested in a bowl, and a stack of bacon waited on a chopping board. "Can I help? Pour coffee, make tea, anything?"

Sarah waved off the offer of help. "All under control. I'll do this and listen while you talk."

Jack, after watching Scott, Layla, and Tammy taking their places at the table, finally moved away from the door, set the radio equipment on the table, and immediately addressed Scott.

"I prefer not to have guns in the house," he said, with a glance over to where his children were gazing at their tablets and tapping away. "I've seen too many accidents. May I look after yours while you're here, sir?"

They all froze, but after a beat, Scott simply nodded and stood up to pull the handgun out from under his jacket. "My apologies. We're not inclined to trust people right now. We didn't mean to abuse your hospitality." He handed it over, butt first.

Nobody looked at Tammy, and she didn't volunteer the fact that she also was carrying. If this guy proved to be a devil in disguise, at least they had one card up their sleeves. Or a gun in one of Tammy's capacious pockets, as the case may be.

"Jack was a sheriff, once," Sarah said while adding bacon to a large pan. "He can usually pick it when someone's carrying."

A warning, perhaps? *Don't mess with Jack; he has contacts in law enforcement?*

Tammy's phone chirped, and she slipped it out of a vest pocket to check her messages. She read the contents, scrolling down, and from the way she tightened her lips, it was clear that it wasn't going to be of any help to them.

"Nothing?" Georgie asked.

"Nothing. Danny says that the thumb drive he found was the last option, and even that was mostly a repeat of what was on the main computer, with a few different names that he has sent through.

Nothing new. I'll just let him know where we are." She tapped out a quick message and then put the phone on the table in front of her.

Jack opened a cupboard above the kitchen counter, placed Scott's gun inside, and closed the door. "You'll have it back when you leave." He nodded at Tammy's phone as he sat down. "You're getting names, locations of survivalists in the area?"

"Yes, here and throughout Kentucky, just in case. The problem is, the kind of people who might have taken Jerry are the types that refuse to have their names on any database. They use fake names, throwaway phones, pay cash, or route payment through a maze." Tammy sighed. "The very measures we use that protect the confidentiality of clients are putting Jerry in danger."

He held out a hand. "May I see the list? I know most of the local survivalists."

Tammy passed him her phone, and he scrolled through the names, every so often nodding slightly. After a few moments, he handed it back. "There are no extremists there that I can see. We've had some of these people in our home, met others at survivalist meets, or chatted online. There are a couple of names there that are very dedicated to what they do, but none that I can see who would harm another." He smiled dryly. "Well, not unless society collapsed. Then all bets are off. They say you don't know what any man is capable of until he's under pressure."

"That's what we're wrestling with all the time—questions about what we would do to protect ourselves; how far would we go," Sarah said over the sound of bacon sizzling in one pan while she cracked eggs into another and put bread into a four-slice toaster. "We like to think that we wouldn't take anything that belonged to someone else if that meant that they were in danger. But there are so many shades of grey."

"As was the case when I was a sheriff," Jack said. "Which is one of the reasons I left."

Georgie studied his face, and then he looked up and met her gaze.

Click. The switch was almost tangible.

He wasn't the one. A wave of relief swept through her. Not only could they relax, but they also had someone who could help.

She glanced at Scott to find him glancing from her to Jack, and in a moment of perfect clarity, she knew he sensed precisely what she did.

"Tammy," she said, "It's not Jack. Let him have your gun."

Jack gave a twisted smile and said, "She can keep it. Right-hand pants pocket, right? Wanted to see what you'd do." He reached under the table, and the next moment there was a gun in his hand, much more serious than hers. "I put this here when we knew you were coming. Can't be too careful."

He returned the weapon to its hiding place and sat back in his chair with his arms folded. "Shall we start again?"

CHAPTER 12

An Upfront Approach

Jack listened to their story attentively while Sarah served up breakfast and drifted over now and then to settle a question for one of her offspring. Georgie began to see that her original view of survivalists hadn't been entirely on target. There were the extremists who stockpiled every weapon known to humanity and acted as though they'd be disappointed if Doomsday didn't arrive. People like Jack and Sarah lived a simple, happy life and simply wanted to give their family the best chance of survival if society went feral.

Luckily, they had been drawn to this family first.

Maybe not *all* luck, she allowed. Through Scott's mother and the crystal ball, they'd followed a cluster of possibilities to end up here.

At first, the four of them skirted around the

reason they had decided to look for Jerry in Marion County, but Jack simply looked at them with his cop face on and asked more questions until Georgie sighed and gave in.

"It will probably sound crazy to you," she said, "but I use a crystal ball. Scott's mother is an astrologer who does card readings. Think what you will, but that's why we're here talking with you now."

"I see." He looked at her thoughtfully. "I've learned to be open-minded. There's more than one survivalist that claims to have seen a vision of the future, and they're not *all* the kind that wear tinfoil on their heads to stop the government from reading their minds."

Sarah, who had been sitting there quietly taking it all in, spoke up. "You have to help them, Jack— but if you get killed, I'll never speak to you again." She touched his hand briefly.

Judging by the smile that touched Jack's lips, it wasn't the first time he'd heard those words. "I'm not about to get killed, Sarah. But you're right; he needs to be stopped."

He? Along with the others, Georgie stared at Jack.

"I know of a few preppers I'd give a wide berth, but only one of them lives close by. He goes by the name of Vincent Cray, but I've called in a few favors over the past few months to find out more about him. He has a criminal background, several aliases, and he sees the survivalist movement more as a ticket to riches than anything else."

"Creepy man," Sarah said with a shudder.

"You've both met him?" Scott asked.

"He came here to introduce himself and offer any help if we needed it, but that wasn't his true agenda. He was after Jack's network of radio operators and to pick his brain about surveillance options."

"I suspect that he's building a database of preppers, and not just to sell them things. There's big money in it." Jack moved restlessly in his chair. "My concern is that you're out of your depth here. He's a dangerous man, and paranoid doesn't begin to describe him."

Tammy sat forward. "But you know where he lives?"

"I've been there. He invited me out to his compound to see his surveillance setup—mostly to get me to think he has nothing to hide, to build trust. It would have worked with most people, but I spotted a couple of cameras he didn't tell me about."

"Can we get onto his property to scout it out,

see if Jerry's there?" She glanced at Georgie. "If we got close, you'd know if he was there, wouldn't you?"

Georgie shrugged helplessly. "I have no idea. You'd think so, but until we get there…"

"He has surveillance cameras in the compound," Jack said. "That's common with preppers with money, but he has more reasons than most to cover up what he's doing. I'd also be betting on sensors and more cameras on all the approaches to the property."

"We have to do something." There was a note of desperation in Tammy's voice. "We can't get this close and not try."

"We still don't know for sure if Jerry's there," Layla pointed out. "What if he's not, and this Vincent catches us trespassing?"

Scott, who had been sitting there mulling things over, said: "We could try an upfront approach. Jack could call him and tell him we've asked for his help, and he thought Vincent might help search. See if he'll talk to us—but a couple of us could go down the road a bit. Go in the back way, check things out."

Jack nodded. "I was thinking along the same lines, arranging a meeting with him. But if I'm taking you there to see him, who's going in the back way? You and Tammy, I'm guessing, since you were the two carrying. But, if you'll excuse me saying so, amateurs can get shot—or shoot other people. How much experience have you had with guns?"

"Target shooting and hunting," Tammy said briefly. "Grew up with guns, won a few tournaments."

Georgie stared at her in amazement. Tammy had won *tournaments*? She just couldn't picture Tammy with a gun, not even dressed as she was today.

"I haven't done as much as Tammy," Scott said. "But I can handle a rifle, and I know a little about handguns."

"If you go in from the fringes of the property and stay well back in the trees at the back fence, you should be right. Just scout it out, see if there's any sign of activity while we talk to Vincent. All right." Jack glanced at his watch. "If Jerry is there, he'll have been in their hands a little less than 24 hours, so the faster we move, the better. Here's the plan."

Less than twenty miles away, Jerry heard the murmur of voices outside before the bolt on the door of his prison rattled. The door swung open, admitting a gust of cold, damp air. He could see rain misting down behind the two figures in the doorway.

Vincent walked over and frowned down at him. He was dressed in camo gear, the same as he had been the day before, but had showered and shaved.

Jerry wouldn't mind a shower himself. A nice long one, with steaming hot water to ease the aches of a night spent on the cold floor of the shipping container.

"You've had a chance to rethink," Vincent said. "Got anything for us yet?"

Jerry had indeed rethought. The picture that kept coming into his mind was a little too bleak for his liking: one very dead Jerry B. Goode versus a handful of names and locations. He had concluded that giving up names in return for his life sounded like a pretty good deal, but not too soon. No, that wasn't the way to negotiate.

"One or two," he said. "You'll have to do some chasing up. My memory's good, but not that good. Most of the details are back at base."

"One or two?" Vincent put his head on one side, regarding him thoughtfully. "You've been designing and selling bug-out vehicles for nearly two years, and that's the best you can do?" He nudged Jerry's foot with the toe of one solid-looking steel-capped boot. "Is it *one* name, Mr. Goode, or is it *two?*"

"Well, two."

"And they are?"

Jerry gave him two names of minor players, people who wouldn't take out a contract on him for violating confidentiality.

"Check them," Vincent said to the man behind him.

It took him about two seconds. "Already have them. Useless. Not what we're after."

Jerry thought fast. "I told you, I can't remember details like that. I have them in a safe place."

"Where?"

"At—" Jerry was about to say 'At home', but an image of these men breaking into his home and finding Tammy flashed into his mind, and he changed it to "At at storage facility."

Vincent said nothing for a moment, then shook his head. "I know that's a lie. You do realize you're making life unnecessarily hard for yourself? Give me the information I want, and nobody ever needs to know it came from you. You can go home and forget all this."

Never scam a scammer, thought Jerry. He knew perfectly well what would happen if he were to agree. Best case scenario: Vincent would let him go and then be back asking for names and details for every new client from then on. Worst case: Jerry B. Goode would disappear from the face of the Earth. He ran through options in his mind.

Maybe he could turn the best case scenario to his advantage.

"We researched you carefully, Mr. Goode. I am quite sure you know the exact location of at least some of those safe houses, Doomsday bunkers, whatever your clients choose to call them, without needing GPS coordinates."

Jerry said nothing. It was clear the guy had something in mind.

He did. "Gary, please restrain Mr. Goode."

The minder behind him came forward.

"Not cable ties again." Jerry tried to keep his voice level. "C'mon, guys. I can't escape from here. Do you need to do that?"

Vincent ignored him, and after judging his companion's size and strength, Jerry didn't attempt to resist. One crack on the head was enough. With a sigh, he held out his hands.

"Behind your back, please."

Every time that pleasant voice issued another command, shivers crawled up Jerry's back. Somehow, the guys that didn't need to shout and bluster were scarier than a muscle-bound bodyguard.

Jerry stood up and turned around, his hands behind his back. When he was incapacitated again, Gary the gorilla finished off the job with duct tape across his mouth.

"I apologize for the discomfort," Vincent said. "We are expecting visitors. Friends of yours, I believe, enquiring after you. We can't have you attracting their attention."

Jerry's pulse leaped, and warring emotions raced through him.

Who? His father? Danny? Who would come after him?

He grunted and widened his eyes, hoping that Vincent would know what he was asking.

"Your sister and a friend of hers." Vincent smiled. "They contacted a local survivalist, and he's bringing them here to see if I can help find you. Unfortunately, I don't believe I'll be able to help, but I'll naturally offer to do everything I can."

He and the gorilla left, and Jerry slumped against the wall, scared out of his mind.

Georgie. Of all people, *Georgie* was here.

He hoped like hell the friend wasn't Tammy.

For Doomsday's sake, why hadn't they brought some real muscle to look for him?

CHAPTER 13

In the House of the Enemy

It had been years since Tammy had crossed rough terrain with a rifle, but it could have been yesterday. The gun's weight felt comfortable and familiar, and she had instinctively returned to the same state of alertness as she used to track and hunt. Some sounds, she knew, were harmless; others had her pausing for a moment, listening.

Scott was a good companion. His eyes, too, were everywhere, and he didn't speak unless it was necessary. He might not have been a hunter, but he had tracked his share of feral animals, it seemed.

Just not the human kind.

Danny's property was shaped like a slice of pie, with the main house at the pointy end near the road. The holding was relatively small, at around

100 acres, but a small creek with slippery rocks and spongy edges made traversing the area more difficult.

"Fresh water," Tammy murmured.

"I noticed. It looks like Mum got that right, at least."

It didn't take them long to reach the small fence that separated the main compound from the rest of the property.

"Not electrified," Scott said softly. As Jack had recommended, they stayed safely in the shelter of the trees and used binoculars to check the place out from a distance of a few hundred yards. "But it would be too easy to breach, so I'm betting on cameras or sensors." He eyed the back of the house, about half a mile distant, just visible through a tangle of trees and scrub. "Let's follow the fence around, see what's there."

Cautiously, they moved from tree to tree, noting the fence's condition and the various outbuildings behind the house. A dozen of them were arranged in a rough arc about halfway between the house and the fence.

"Pity we can't see the front of them," Scott muttered, looking at a large barn and the wall of a carport that currently sheltered three vehicles: a troop carrier and a couple of 4WDs. "Those shipping containers are probably full of supplies and weapons. He sounds like the type to have an arsenal."

Tammy eyed the containers. "Jerry could be in any of them."

"Or the main house. Or," Scott pointed to a large metal trapdoor in front of the barn, "down there. Some kind of storm cellar or bunker."

Tammy stared at the trapdoor. If Jerry was there, how were they going to get him out? They'd be exposed the moment they walked over to it. "We may have to come back at night."

"Won't help. I can see dogs over there in the kennels—see, on the right." He handed her the binoculars. "They'll be guarding the yard at night."

They kept moving, using binoculars to check the outbuildings and what they could see of the house until they reached the side fence. The end of the arc put them close to the house and the road, and peering back; they could just see the front of the containers. They all had heavy-duty bolts and padlocks.

Tammy leaned against a tree and thought. She might be able to shoot, but hunting was very different from trying to break into a fenced compound with dogs and sensors and cameras to rescue someone who was being held God knew where. "What are we going to do?"

"What you're going to do," said a voice behind them, "is drop those rifles and turn around real slow."

Inside the house, Georgie and Layla were sitting on the edge of a sofa, sipping tea provided by their hostess, while Jack explained their situation to Vincent.

The woman Vincent had introduced as his wife, Alice, sat quietly to one side, her gaze moving from one of them to the other. A small, nondescript woman with chin-length auburn hair, she gave the impression of being the weaker half of the couple, but Georgie knew instinctively it was a front. It probably suited Vincent's purposes to have a wife that looked non-threatening.

Vincent kept attentive eyes on Jack while he talked, occasionally interjecting. When had the GPS coordinates cut out? What had brought them to Marion? What did they intend to do next? On the last question, his eyes flicked to Georgie, obviously directing it at her.

"We're trying to decide what to do. We found Jack on a forum, but he said you were probably the one around here with the most expertise." A bit of flattery never hurt, she thought.

Vincent gave her a polite smile. "Forgive me, but I still don't understand why you're in Marion County. You said there was a possible sighting of your brother. Who and where?"

Georgie exchanged a look with Layla. If she told him the truth, he might think she was a complete flake. But he was right: what other reason did they have for being here? Her bad-guy radar flagged him as being about as trustworthy as a piranha.

It wouldn't surprise her in the least to discover that Jerry was around here somewhere, stashed away out of sight. The thought panicked her. She'd honestly thought that if Jerry were close by, she'd sense it. She'd *know*.

She wasn't picking up anything. If he was here, he wasn't sending out any vibes.

Georgie hoped that wasn't a bad sign.

"Ma'am?" Vincent prompted, still polite.

Nothing ventured, nothing gained. "The sighting was mine. I'm a psychic," she said, which she thought might sound just a tad more authentic than a gypsy fortune-teller. It didn't, judging by the swiftly camouflaged reaction on Vincent's face.

"You're a *psychic?*"

"Yes." She omitted any mention of Scott's mother's contribution. An astrologer from Australia pitching in would sound too looney-tunes for words.

"Are you saying that you had some sort of vision of your brother in Marion County?"

"Not specifically," she said. "I got the sense that he might be somewhere around the middle of Kentucky, and Marion happens to be the geographic center. We Googled preppers in the area and found Jack, and he brought us to you." She shrugged. "I already know how it must sound. But here we are, and considering that his last coordinates—well, the vehicle's coordinates anyway— were in northern Kentucky, I'm not too far out."

"You hope," he said.

"That's right. I hope." She schooled her face into an expression of neutrality. "You don't have to help. Jack probably knows more people he can ask."

"That I do," Jack agreed. "But Vincent's the most experienced."

"If you think we're way off base, that's fine," she said, knowing her voice telegraphed that it was anything but fine. "We'll keep moving."

"I didn't say I wouldn't help." His phone gave two short beeps, and he extracted it from his pocket. "Excuse me."

He glanced at the screen, stared at it impassively for a moment, and then tapped out a short message before putting the phone away again. "Sorry. People are always contacting me for advice." He looked at his wife. "Can you make more coffee, Alice? Gary will be here in a moment."

Without saying anything, his wife got to her feet and drifted off to the kitchen. The perfect submissive wife. *Not.*

Georgie turned her attention back to Vincent. "What would *you* suggest we do next?" She was on edge, every nerve ending humming. She didn't trust this guy any more than his wife. The sooner they were out of there, the better, but they had to give Scott and Tammy as much time as possible to check things out.

Vincent stared at her, and meeting his dark, shrewd eyes, Georgie felt an icy tremor go up her spine.

This was the one. She didn't know where her brother was, but *this* was the man responsible for his disappearance.

She waited until Vincent looked away before

she caught Jack's eye. His face showed absolutely no emotion, but he jumped in immediately.

"I think we need to divide our efforts. I'll get in touch with a few people I trust on the forum to see if they've heard or seen anything. Vincent, you'll know people that I don't. Can you do the same?"

He nodded. "Will you all be going back to your place?"

What, so we can all be sitting ducks? thought Georgie. No chance.

"I can't just go back and sit around," she said quickly. "Jack, can you line up someone who will talk with us? You never know what I might pick up face to face."

Vincent looked skeptical. "How will that help you find your brother any better than a phone conversation?"

"I can't look into people's eyes on the phone." She stared at him challengingly.

Vincent smiled smoothly and pointed two fingers at his own eyes. "So what do you see here?"

"I see a man who doesn't trust anyone," she said quietly. "You think it protects you, but it could be your downfall."

For a moment, something feral flickered at the back of his gaze, making her heart pound. *Way to go, Georgie. Poke a stick at the snake, why don't you.*

He kept a neutral expression. "That's my official fortune told, is it? Well, we'll see. Given the way your brother disappeared, I wouldn't be too quick to trust people if I were you. Call me paranoid."

"We do appreciate your help," she said stiffly. "Jack, would you mind terribly if we moved quickly on this? The more time passes, the less chance we have of finding Jerry." She bent down to pick up her bag. "I hope you don't think we're rude, leaving so quickly. I just feel that time is slipping away."

Vincent nodded and stood up, and at the same time, she heard a door open somewhere nearby. They listened to a low murmur from Vincent's wife and the rumble of a man's voice in response. It sounded like Gary had arrived for his coffee.

Heavy footsteps came toward them. Georgie frowned. More than one set of footsteps…

Georgie sat forward. With an awful feeling of dread, she knew what she would see even before anyone appeared.

Scott and Tammy were pushed into the room by a mountain of muscle carrying not one but two rifles, one of them right in the middle of Tammy's back.

Scott's face was tight with anger and frustration. Tammy seemed to be equal parts scared and furious.

"Welcome to the party," Vincent said from his position over near the window. When Georgie looked at him, she saw that a handgun had magically appeared in his hand, and he was watching Jack carefully. "Jack, I'm afraid you've been holding out on me. You brought me four visitors, not two."

CHAPTER 14
Captured

Jerry was half glad and half sorry to hear someone outside his miserable prison: forty minutes of sitting in a cold, damp shipping container waiting for the gorilla to return had given him way too much time to think. He wasn't at all sure that he'd be able to talk his way out of this.

His arms were killing him from the way they'd wrenched them behind his back so they could lash his hands together, and behind the duct tape, his mouth was dry and swollen.

He would give up the names—some names—and deal with the fallout later. The problem was, he didn't want to reveal where he kept his records, which was on a single-purpose laptop he kept stowed at the bottom of Tammy's giant retro goodies cupboard in his cavernous garage. She had everything in there from lengths of fabric to delicate china sets and frilly aprons.

He didn't want this crew anywhere near Tammy.

The door swung open, and a body was shoved in, landing on the floor near Jerry. It was a man in his thirties, trussed up with cable ties. He swore and wrenched himself onto his side, furious, struggling to sit up.

The gorilla advanced a few steps, gave the newcomer a solid kick, and reached down to haul Jerry to his feet. "Up. Get moving." He shoved Jerry through the door, closed it and shot the bolt, and then pushed him across the gravel backyard towards the house.

Damn, damn, damn. How had he gotten himself into this? And what now?

He could hear Rosa's voice echoing through the years. How many times had she fixed him with that black stare of hers and told him to shape up? *Don't lie to me, young Jerry. You're up to no good again with those friends of yours. Lie down with dogs, and you get up with fleas.*

Well, he was with a pack of rabid dogs now.

The gorilla opened the back door and guided him through a kitchen. There was a slight-looking woman with ginger hair in there, banging pots and pans. She barely spared him a glance, as though it was an everyday occurrence to have a gagged captive manhandled through her house.

Then he was in the living room, and his heart dropped. Sitting on the sofa opposite, Tammy looked directly at him, her big blue eyes wide with apprehension. Beside her, Scott's usually calm face was set in a rigid mask.

Huddled together on another sofa were Georgie and Layla.

Oh hell, hell, hell. *All four of them.*

Jerry's knees felt oddly weak.

"Jerry!" Tammy's hand went to her mouth at the sight of him, and she started to get up, but Vincent, standing by casually with a rifle in his hand, shoved her back again.

Jerry, restrained by two hundred pounds of muscle and steroids, couldn't get to her. He grunted and looked wildly at Vincent.

"Take off the tape," Vincent said mildly. "He might be prepared to talk now."

Looking as though he enjoyed it, the gorilla ripped off the tape, taking hair and skin with it.

"Now that I have something you want," Vincent said, "do you think we might revisit those locations?"

The moment she saw Jerry stumble into the room, Tammy was seized by two conflicting emotions: enormous relief because he was alive and a quickly growing fury because of the way he'd been treated.

Cold fury she could work with. It was an emotion she'd felt many times around her father and brothers. All at once, the fear was gone.

After the first involuntary look of shock at seeing her, Jerry had schooled his face into an expression of mild resentment. "Since we're being civilized, and you have enough firepower to start a war," he said, "Can we ditch the cable ties?" He half-turned, offering his hands to his minder.

All eyes were on Jerry, so Tammy took the opportunity to nudge Scott's knee with hers. Without looking at her, he returned the pressure.

On the other side of the room, Georgie and Layla were watching them.

If a chance presented itself, they would take it. Vincent and the big guy he called Gary had taken possession of their rifles and the handguns, but Tammy still had a compact pistol attached to her ankle. They had taken the stun gun from Scott, unfortunately, but he could still fight.

She just hoped that Layla and Georgie were

concealing a weapon or two. Even a hairpin was better than nothing.

All they needed was a chance.

Standing beside Gary, Jerry kept his expression neutral while trying to figure out how he might get out of this. On the surface, it looked hopeless – but he'd talked his way out of tricky situations in the past. Not as tough as this one, admittedly, but Jerry B. Goode wasn't one to give up.

"Cut the ties," Vincent ordered. He raised the gun and squinted along his arm theatrically, using Jerry's head as the target. "Good of your friends to donate some more weaponry to the cause. It's loaded, by the way. I wouldn't make any sudden moves."

"I don't intend to," Jerry said, unable to quell a flinch at the sight of the business end of a gun barrel pointed his way. He sighed with relief as his hands were cut free. "That's better."

"You'd better believe one thing," Vincent said, keeping the gun firmly on Jerry. "I'm not going to mess around. You know what I want. And—" he swung the weapon around until it was aimed at Tammy, and then let it describe an arc that encompassed Georgie and Layla too, "—you know I'll stop at nothing to get it. So, shall we start?"

Now that Tammy was right where he could see her, Jerry figured that he had nothing to lose by telling him. "At my house."

"*Where* at your house?"

Here we go, Jerry thought. Time to see if he could turn the best-case scenario to his advantage. "Before I tell you," he said, "let me ask you how big you want this to grow. Keep in mind that new preppers turn up or contact us every day. We're selling bug-out vehicles of all sizes like there's going to be an Apocalypse tomorrow. You want names; we've got them. Not just the ones I've got *now*, but all those in the future." He rubbed his chin.

Tammy, bless her heart, picked up on the cue right away. So she should; she was the one who had pointed out that she always knew when he was up to no good because of that very gesture. She pasted an appropriate expression of disdain on her face and butted in.

"Jerry, no. It's not right. Those people *trust* us. You can't do a deal with this guy."

"If I don't do a deal, Tams, we'll be dead," he said bluntly.

"Now you're showing some sense." Vincent

lowered the gun a fraction. "Sit on that chair and keep your hands where I can see them."

"I don't *believe* this, Jerry." Tammy made an expansive gesture of disgust and hitched herself forward on the sofa, looking as though she wanted to launch herself at her boyfriend. "The Johnny B. Goode RV Empire prides itself on ethical business practices." She jerked a thumb at Georgie. "Your sister and I have a really good name in the industry. Now you're going to tell this—this *crook* where he can find the vehicles that we sold people in good faith?"

Jerry had done as he was bid and taken a seat on the edge of a recliner chair. "It's not so much about the vehicles. He wants to know where the bunkers are. The safe houses."

"Yes, that's what he told me," said Tammy with pursed lips and a reproving look at Vincent. She tugged off her cap and shook out her blonde curls, immediately looking more like a blonde bimbo. "I told him there was no way you would give them up."

Beside her, Scott said in a reasoning voice, "Tammy, love, you have to be practical. We tried it your way to get Jerry back and look what happened. You're out of your league here. Just do the deal."

Tammy glared at him and then at Vincent. "Well, I don't think—"

"Just shut up, will you?" Losing patience, Vincent whipped around and took a step toward her. Tammy shrieked, defensively pulling both feet up on the sofa, looking up at him with scared blue eyes.

"Not another word out of you. Go back home and play house with your pretty little trailers."

"OK, OK!" She bit her lip and her eyes filled with tears.

Scott pretended impatience with her. "The sooner you do what you're told, the sooner this will all be over. Can you just stop it?"

"Yes," she said in a small voice, not looking at him.

I love that girl, thought Jerry. He never thought he'd find anyone who could play people as well as he could.

Whoever the submissive girl sitting on the sofa was, it wasn't the real Tammy.

When Vincent stopped glaring at her and turned his attention back to Jerry, Tammy quickly checked everyone's position in the room. She didn't want to shoot one of her friends by mistake.

Beside her, Scott was ready: Tammy could feel it. She nudged him with her toe, an easy move with her feet up on the seat.

Over on the other side of the room, Jerry looked defeated, but she knew that he too would be ready to spring into action.

Georgie and Layla were covertly watching her. She hoped that Layla still had that stun gun on her.

Now, she thought, and let one hand move toward her ankle, where the reassuring weight of the gun rested against her sock.

Now.

CHAPTER 15

Fighting for Life

Vincent kept the rifle trained on Jerry. "You've given us a lot more housekeeping than we would wish. Now we have to do something about Jack, which will provide us with quite a few problems. Not to mention your sister." His eyes flicked to Georgie. "It's a great pity your crystal ball didn't tell you to stay at home. Clearly, you didn't get to see *your* future. Gary, would you kindly restrain Ms. Goode and her friend here?"

Gary grunted and lumbered towards them, a bag of cable ties in one huge paw.

Without waiting to be told, Georgie held out both hands, wrists together. Tammy watched closely, her hand poised near her ankle. Was Georgie *helping* them?

Almost immediately, she understood what Georgie was doing. As she sat forward, offering her hands to Gary, she partially obscured Layla. Tammy saw the quick flash of Layla's hand dipping into a pocket, and then something in her hand sparked and crackled.

Gary roared and collapsed like a house of cards, and the stun gun that Layla held crackled again. Vincent swore and lifted the rifle, aiming it directly at Jerry. "Alice!" he roared. "Gun!"

While his attention was on Jerry, Tammy slid her gun out of its hiding place. Vincent's knee was less than a body length from her and at eye level.

"Jerry, duck!" she yelled a half-second before she shot Vincent in the knee.

Jerry flung himself off to one side and immediately tripped on the rug, with one arm windmilling wildly as he tried to stop the fall. At the same time, Vincent screamed, jerking his rifle so it discharged into Jerry's arm, right where his head had been a second before.

Jerry scrambled up, not appearing to notice his injury, and threw himself across the room at Vincent. Scott tackled him from the other side.

Tammy heard a shriek from the doorway, and there was Alice, with yet another handgun. For a moment, she stared at the flailing bodies on the floor, her hand wildly swinging back and forth as though trying to decide whom to shoot.

Tammy snatched Scott's rifle from where it leaned against the wall and raised it, aiming straight at Alice. "Put it down!"

Alice didn't bat an eyelid. She just took a few steps back and kept her gun pointed at the writhing bodies on the floor, flicking a glance at Tammy. "I'll shoot them."

Tammy bowed to the inevitable. For the second time in five minutes, after not firing a gun for seven years, she aimed and hit her target exactly where she wanted. Alice wailed like a banshee, and her weapon flew up into the air, flipping over before it crashed to the ground.

Tammy closed her eyes and finally breathed.

Good thing she wasn't shooting to kill.

CHAPTER 16

An Ultimatum

Four weeks later, Georgie and Scott slipped into the massive marquee at the Happy Days Retro Rally to take their seats next to Layla in the front row. Getting into the spirit of things, Georgie had left her gypsy outfits back in the trailer and was wearing much the same as Layla: a poodle skirt with a close-fitting blouse and a long-line cardigan —and the obligatory saddle shoes, of course.

"Payback time," said Layla with satisfaction, jigging her knee to a fifties rock tune. "Tammy will love this."

"Oh yeah," said Georgie. "Although, of course, Jerry's playing for the sympathy card with his arm. Fonzie in a cast."

"Ever the bad boy," murmured Layla. She leaned across Georgie. "What about you, Scott?

When are we going to get you into retro? Up on the stage, performing?"

"Performing, never," he said comfortably. "And I *am* in retro."

Layla eyed his khaki pants and button-down plaid shirt. "You can't count that."

"Can too," he returned. "I Googled it. Richie Cunningham to a T." He pointed at his neat hair. "Even to the good-boy hair."

Georgie heaved a sigh. "Don't you know that every girl dreams of running away with the *bad* boy?"

"What, like Jerry?"

"Ouch," she said. "All right, I take it back. But one day I'm going to meet your brother, and he's going to tell me all your secrets. There's *got* to be some misbehavior in your background somewhere."

"Speaking of bad boys," he said, nodding at the stage.

The MC was walking onstage, with all the finalists behind him. The Joanies, the Fonzies, the Richies, Mr. Cunningham, Mrs. Cunningham, and a couple of Pinky Tuscadero lookalikes.

Jerry made just as good a Fonzie as he did a Danny Zuko. His appearance was greeted by a storm of clapping, which was as much to do with his hero status for surviving a prepper abduction as it was for being a retro icon.

Jerry grinned, smoothed his free hand over his pompadour hairstyle, and raised the arm in a cast to the crowd. More clapping.

"Oh man," Georgie said. "The size of his ego just increased even more."

Every contestant had the chance to ham it up for the audience until finally, the best two in each category were lined up across the stage.

"And now," the MC said, "for the winners! Step forward when I call your name and collect your prize!

Nobody was surprised when Tammy, skipping forward as a wide-eyed innocent Joanie, collected one of the prizes. It was even less of a surprise when Jerry won the Fonzie competition—and when the two of them stepped forward to have a photo taken together, the place erupted. Tammy Dyson, one of their favorite contestants, and Jerry B. Goode, the heir apparent of the most popular manufacturer of vintage-look trailers.

He looked much better as Fonzie, Georgie decided, than as a prepper carrying a rifle and defending himself against a couple of crazies.

The band struck up the "Happy Days" theme while willing hands folded chairs and stacked them out of the way, ready for a night of fun on the dance floor.

"It'll take them hours to be free of this bunch," Scott observed. "Guess all we can do is join in and enjoy the party." He patted Georgie on the arm. "You haven't seen me dance. There's a treat in store."

Somehow, judging by the devilish glint in his eyes, she doubted it.

Much later that night, they all met up in Jerry's RV. It mightn't be to their taste as much as retro trailers, but there was no doubt that it offered more space for social get-togethers.

Georgie walked in and then stopped and looked around. The RV still had its elements of black and gold, but it was…different. Some extra cushions in shades of taupe and latte lay onto the charcoal leather seats, and tasteful artwork graced the wall. The overall effect softened the original black and gold and made it look much homier.

She nodded approvingly. "I see Tammy's had a hand in this."

"Got it in one," agreed Tammy. "He had it

looking like a mix between a hotel lobby and a Hugh Hefner bunny trap."

"How did you do it?" Georgie accepted a glass of bubbly from Jerry. "The number of times I tried to convince him that all that glitz didn't work—but would he listen to his sister?"

Jerry patted her on the head. "Never have in the past; why would I start now?"

She swiped at him half-heartedly. He still annoyed her more often than not, but it was only when she had faced the possibility of losing him that she had to admit that he had captured some tiny corner of her heart. OK, it might be a teeny tiny corner all covered in dust and cobwebs, but it was Jerry's corner.

And he *had* improved since Tammy had come into his life. Who knew what the future might hold?

"What?" Jerry said, casting her a suspicious look. "You're doing that weird grin again. I don't trust you when you look like that."

"No reason," Georgie said. "Daydreaming. I was a million miles away."

Jerry cocked his head and looked at her, waiting, but she just smiled some more. Give Jerry an inch, and he'd take a mile. Tell him that he was improving? Not any time soon.

"Once upon a time," he said, giving up and handing out more glasses of champagne, "you used to be a lot easier to handle. Ever since you ran away to join the gypsies, there's no knowing what you'll do next." He gave Tammy the last glass and bent over to plant a swift kiss on her lips before turning to address them all, remaining on his feet. "Anyway…" he cleared his throat. "I just thought I'd take the occasion to say thank you all for coming to rescue me. I know what I owe you. I want to propose a toast to the Crystal Ball Team." He held up his glass and waited.

"Crystal Ball *Investigation* Team," Tammy corrected him. "CBI. Slick operation like ours, it's important to get the name right." She raised her glass.

It was Georgie's turn. "And to Scott's mother, for pointing us in the right direction. An honorary member of the team. To Tammy, who can handle a rifle as well as any prepper. And Layla, a demon with the stun gun." She pretended disappointment. "I *would* have taken somebody out with the pepper spray, but you guys didn't leave me any work to do."

"All I got to do was tackle Vincent, but that was satisfying," Scott observed with a grin. "Anyway, here's to all of us—and Jerry, for keeping his cool."

They all raised their glasses and drank, but

there was a hint of reserve in the air. Nobody had enjoyed coming so close to real danger.

Jerry sat down next to Tammy. "There's a bit more news. Two bits." He looked around, stretching out the moment, enjoying the air of expectancy. "First: Danny Howell has been arrested."

"*Danny*?" Georgie was stunned. "Danny from the Bugout Base? Danny, who did the search for us on the computer?"

"The very one." Jerry's face, as usual, held no clue to his feelings; that was why he was such an excellent poker player. He could act any part or show nothing. "I started thinking: how come the satellite tracker stopped working? We camouflage them in a different place in each vehicle; sometimes, we have two in case one is removed. Vincent knew where it was, but I didn't see him disable it. He didn't remove it either—I know, because I was in the back of it for hours before we got to Marion. So that means that either they disabled the software, or someone was helping them from our end."

"And Danny was the one monitoring the satellite tracker," Scott said. "He was the one feeding us information from back at the base."

Georgie thought of the useless lists that Danny had given them. "He didn't give us anyone that might help—nobody that wasn't already easy to find online."

"If you remember," Tammy said, "he sent us Jack's name as one of the final three—but only when he knew we were heading to Marion. Looking as though he was helpful."

"So Danny was keeping Vincent informed all along." Georgie felt a heavy sense of betrayal that someone in the Johnny B. Goode RV Empire would sell them out like that.

"He knew exactly who was coming after me the whole time," Jerry agreed. "So when Jack turned up at his house with just two of you, he knew the others were out there somewhere."

Scott snapped his fingers. "So that's how Vincent's favorite gorilla found us out there. It didn't matter how careful we were being."

"Pity I didn't get to shoot him as well," Tammy said, her blue eyes suddenly stormy. "I'm glad you stunned him twice, Layla."

"Three times." Layla pretended nonchalance while she studied her fingernails. "He was a big boy. I wanted to make sure I got it right."

"Well, they're all in prison now." Jerry cleared his throat. "Which brings me to the second bit of news. Since this has highlighted major security problems with our database for bug-out vehicles and details of shelters for preppers, we have a huge new business opportunity: we will specialize in secure systems and emergency communications. Just something more we can offer to our clients. Which will mean even greater expansion." He shook a playful finger at Georgie and then rested his hand on Tammy's knee. "But don't worry, girls, your vintage division won't suffer."

Tammy put down her glass. She exchanged a glance with Georgie and then picked up Jerry's hand as though it were a dead fish and deposited it back on his knee. Then she sat back, folded her arms, and just looked at him.

Jerry looked from her to his sister. "What? I'm not doing this at the expense of your division; I just told you. Vintage is quite safe."

"Vintage might be safe," Tammy said. "But are *we*? You said you were going to step *back* from the prepper extremists."

"Well, I am. No more going out alone to meet them. No more demos at remote locations. I told you that."

"And now," Georgie said, "you are going to specialize in security. And communications. Secret squirrel stuff. Right?"

"There's an opening. We have to take it." Jerry gave her his best I-can't-believe-you-can't-see-this face, followed by his most engaging smile. "If we don't step in—and make the most of the publicity we've got—then someone else will."

"Fine." Georgie set down her glass with a *thunk* that set the crystal ringing. "Let someone else do it. You can make enough money from everything else we do."

"I *can't*. I've already set things in motion. I've made promises." He gave up on Georgie and focused on Tammy. "I'll be careful. I don't want to get shot again."

"If you go ahead with this, it won't be the preppers you have to worry about," Tammy said pointedly. "So you've made some promises. You made promises to us too. Did you forget?"

"Tams." He looked hunted. If Georgie hadn't been so annoyed with him, she would have enjoyed his discomfiture.

"Rosa was right," Tammy said. "She said as a boy you were always up to no good. Always plotting, always planning the next scheme. She says there's hope for you, but sometimes I wonder." She tapped the cast on his arm. "You got out of it lightly this time. Forget this idea, Jerry, or I'm out."

He stared at her.

Everybody else found something interesting to hold their attention while they waited.

After a moment, Jerry said, "What kind of out?"

"Out of your life, Jerry." Tammy held his eye firmly. "I *shot* people for you. I swore I'd never shoot a living creature again, but I did it for you. I'll never do it again."

Jerry drew in a deep breath.

He stood up and walked across to stare out of the RV door at the lights from trailers and the late-night groups strumming guitars or laughing over stories.

Their scene, thought Georgie, watching him. Their incredible, safe, happy retro scene. The life she and Tammy and Layla loved.

Jerry tapped his fingers on the doorframe. Then he turned, shrugged, and opened his hands outward, the cast on his arm making the gesture awkward. "OK. I'll outsource it. Just as we do now."

Tammy raised an eyebrow.

He said stiffly, "I'm sorry. I really am sorry, Tams." He held her gaze, and they could all see the tic in his jaw while he waited.

Wow, thought Georgie. *I think he is.*

Tammy made him suffer for another few seconds and then relented. "OK."

"Tams?" He held out his arms, and she bounced up and walked into a hug.

Georgie let out a pent-up breath. Her poker-faced brother hadn't been able to hide his genuine emotions when it counted.

He wasn't stupid enough to let Tammy go.

Maybe he wasn't *always* up to no good.

Well, now you know a little more about Tammy… and after going head to head with the preppers, I think Jerry may be a tad chastened by his experiences! (But just wait, he'll bounce back later in the series. You just can't keep a guy like Jerry down.)

In our next story, *In Good Hands*, Georgie gives in to her father's requests to take part in a documentary about the Goode family's RV adventures. She wasn't keen to start with, and when she meets the presenter, Jaxx Saxby, her heart sinks like a stone. Unfortunately, much as she doesn't like Jaxx, the producer is in trouble… and only Georgie can help! (You can read a preview chapter of **In Good Hands** in this book.)

Here's an invitation for you: subscribe to my newsletter to get news of new releases, bonus books, specials and a sneak peek at scenes from my books in progress. As a welcome gift, you'll also receive a copy of *Fortune's Wheel*, the prequel to the Georgie series.

Here's your chance to find out more about the intriguing old woman that Georgie sees as a kind of taciturn genie. Whether she wanted to believe it or not, from birth Georgie was destined to follow in

Great-Grandma Rosa's footsteps—as well as inherit her crystal ball!

If you haven't already done so, visit my website below to join other readers and download your copy.

MargMcAlister.com/free-georgie-book/

ABOUT THE AUTHOR

Marg McAlister is the author of the popular Georgie B. Goode Cozy Mystery series (set in the USA) and Series 2 (Australian RV Adventure series), also featuring Georgie.

Marg lives by the sea on the mid-north coast of NSW, but she and her husband spend part of the year on The Gemfields in Central Queensland, living off the grid on their mining claim. While her husband digs for sapphires and zircons, operates the wash plant and drives around dirt tracks, Marg is usually writing—or socializing!

Marg is also the author of a series of books for aspiring writers, and the owner of Blue Gem Publishing, which publishes books in a range of genres.

IN GOOD HANDS

Chapter 1

Jaxx Saxby frowned at Georgie and shook an admonishing finger back and forth in front of her nose. "Don't look at the camera. Look at me."

"Oh. Sorry." Georgie forced a smile and wondered whether it was too late to change her mind. She fought down a wild urge to jump up from the seat, hurtle down the steps of her gypsy trailer and keep going.

Unfortunately, it was very much too late.

Her father had not only agreed to this cable TV special about his gargantuan Johnny B. Goode RV Empire; he was more enthusiastic than he'd been about anything *ever*. From the moment Jaxx Saxby had sashayed into his office and said, "We'd like to feature you on our cable TV show "From Little Things"—you've heard of it, of course?" he was putty in her hands. He'd not only heard of the show that traced the growth of successful businesses from humble beginnings; he had often commented that *his* business deserved to be on it.

Now Johnny B. Goode had checked off something else on his bucket list, and at the tail end of the shoot, it was finally Georgie's turn to be interviewed. So here she was, stuck with one of the most annoying people she had ever met, being forced to perform for the cameras.

Georgie sneaked another look at the woman sitting opposite while she was flipping through some sort of running sheet. With her artfully tossed auburn hair, botoxed lips, and figure-hugging outfits, she was a hair's breadth away from looking more like a porn star than a TV presenter, but it seemed to work with the viewers.

If she bolted, Georgie was sure that Jaxx would chase right after her—or, more likely, bark an imperious command to her producer, Lilli Chin Lee, and send *her* in hot pursuit.

She cast an eye at the crystal ball, hidden under its black velvet cloth, waiting to be unveiled. Another surge of panic hit. What if it didn't work while the cameras were on her? What if she looked like a complete fraud?

Lilli leaned forward from where she was propped against the cooktop opposite the table and pointed at the pink pig next to Georgie's elbow. "What's that? Can we move it? It doesn't add to the atmosphere."

"It's my donation piggy bank." Feeling the color

rising in her cheeks, Georgie grabbed the pig and passed it to the producer.

Lilli tilted the pig and read the note stuck to its belly. "*Donations to Red Cross.* What, you mean you do readings for *free*?"

"Yes. Well, just a donation, but how much is up to the customer."

"Then how do you make any money?"

"I don't." Feeling hunted, Georgie looked around for help, but her gypsy trailer was filled with strangers, cameras, and cables. No friends in sight: Layla and Tammy were outside waiting to be debriefed after it was all over.

"There could be an angle in that," Lilli said to Jaxx. "Ask the question in the interview."

"No, please don't." The last thing Georgie wanted to do was launch into an explanation of why and how she had started asking for donations instead of charging for a consultation—which was mostly because she didn't want to be labeled a shyster. "It's a personal thing."

"Hmm." Jaxx pursed her lips. "Oh well, I suppose you don't want a stream of freeloaders all turning up to have their fortunes read."

"It's not that. I don't do a lot of it." Georgie changed the subject. "So, what are we going to talk about?"

Jaxx waved a languid hand at her producer. "Lilli? Do you have the questions prepared?"

"Don't I always?" Lilli said sweetly, but Georgie didn't miss the brief flash of irritation in her eyes.

"Cheat sheets ready?"

"Of course." Lilli exchanged a look with Seth, the cameraman standing next to her, peering through the lens. They didn't actually roll their eyes, but Georgie could feel it.

The cameraman adjusted his headphones. "Soundcheck. You first, Jaxx."

"Testing, testing, one two three," she said in a bored voice. "I'm interviewing, um," she paused to glance at the paper in front of her, "Georgie, gypsy fortune-teller, daughter of Johnny B. Goode."

Great. An interviewer who couldn't even remember her name.

"That's fine." The cameraman gave a thumbs-up. "Now you, Georgie."

"Testing one two three," she said obligingly. "Being interviewed by, um," she drummed her fingers on the table as though trying to remember, "Jaxx Saxby."

It all went completely over Jaxx's head, but Lilli bit back a smile.

"Are we all ready, then?" Jaxx took a deep breath and flipped out the ends of her hair before addressing Georgie. "You don't need to worry if you fluff a line. Seth can do as many takes as necessary."

"Having said that," Lilli put in, "the fewer takes we need, the better."

Nervousness curled in Georgie's stomach. This was all utterly alien to her usual quiet environment, with a gently flickering candle in the background. Today she was trying not to squint into the glare of the portable lights.

"I usually light a candle," she said. "But it wouldn't have any effect with all these lights."

"We can do fill-ins later," Seth told her. "Different angles, close-up shots, that kind of thing. Ready to begin?"

"As ready as we'll ever be," Jaxx said. "Lilli? Questions?"

"Got them here," Lilli said, holding up a sheet of paper. She stood to one side of Georgie, out of view of the camera, but Jaxx could see her prompts. "Start with the usual intro."

Georgie turned slightly to read what was on the paper. It said:

GEORGIE B. GOODE
(DAUGHTER)
GYPSY FORTUNE TELLER

CRYSTAL BALL
GREAT-GRANDMA ROSA

"Georgie! Look at *me*, remember?" Jaxx said sharply. "Not Lilli. Not the camera. They're not *there*, all right?"

Georgie looked guiltily back at Jaxx. "Sorry."

"After three," Seth said. "Three, two, one…and we're rolling."

Jaxx beamed at the camera, waited for a beat, and then said brightly: "You might think that an RV business is all about motorhomes, modern trailers, and fifth wheels, but that's not the case with Johnny. B. Goode's family. His daughter, Georgie, has followed a different path. She has taken to the road in a colorful gypsy trailer and earns a living telling fortunes with her grandma Rosa's crystal ball. We're going to…"

Georgie held up a hand. "Wait—sorry, but that's not quite right. I don't earn a living through telling fortunes, remember. And it's my *great* grand-mother, not my grandmother."

"Cut," Seth said.

Jaxx groaned and smacked herself on the fore-head. "Georgie. You'll have a chance to have your say in a moment. That was just the *intro.*"

"I know, I'm sorry," Georgie said hastily. "But

I *don't* earn a living doing this, so it would be wrong to say I do. And, well, Rosa is my father's grandmother, not mine."

"You could change that to "has people lining up", Lilli said to Jaxx. "As in: "she has taken to the road, yadda yadda yadda, and people are lining up to have their fortunes told. With her *great* grandma's crystal ball.""

"I suppose so." Jaxx looked a mite petulant about having Lilli tell her what to do, regardless of whether it was the producer's job. "Let's try again. Georgie, please, try to remember you're in good hands here. We've done this a thousand times before, so just go along with what we say."

"When you're ready," Seth said. "Three, two, one...rolling."

Lilli went through her spiel again, ending with: "...and now we're going to find out more about what happens when a gypsy looks into a crystal ball. Georgie, let's imagine that I'm coming to you to have my fortune told. What happens next?"

"I usually wait to see what you will say," Georgie said. "Some people come right out and tell me what they want to know. Others are happy to let it roll along and see what I come up with."

"I'll go with letting it roll along," Jaxx said. She flicked her hair again and leaned forward conspiratorially. "I *might* be interested to know whether you see any tall, dark strangers coming into my life." She gave a low, throaty chuckle. "But if you foresee any airline crashes that involve me, keep it to yourself!"

"You should know that using a crystal ball is not like switching on a computer," Georgie told her. "I can't tap into some magical database in the sky." She slowly drew the cloth off the crystal ball, which instantly reflected the glare of the powerful lights. "In fact, at times it's like dealing with a stubborn teenager. I can sit here with questions in mind, and be met with the equivalent of a blank look."

Jaxx laughed for the camera. "I hope that doesn't happen today. I'm curious. Show me what you do."

"I start by holding a question in my mind. In this case, let's make it general: *'What does the future hold for Jaxx Saxby?'*" Georgie drew the crystal ball slightly closer and gently closed her hands around it. "I'd like you to keep the same question in your mind, Jaxx. Or anything else that you want to know."

"OK." Jaxx waited for five seconds, watching her, and then said, "What happens when you put your hands on the crystal ball? Does that make a difference?"

As long as the person with me doesn't keep talking, Georgie wanted to say. Instead, she said, "It seems to help create some sort of connection." She shut out Jaxx and closed her eyes. *What does the future hold for Jaxx Saxby…?*

"Do you feel anything when you do that?"

"I often feel a sensation of warmth."

"Is that what you're feeling now?"

"Yes." Somehow, despite Jaxx and her interruptions, Georgie *was* detecting the familiar sensation of her skin becoming warmer. There was a flicker of something in her mind.

Relieved, she almost huffed out a sigh of relief. She should be able to satisfy the woman with some small insight. She wanted to come up with something that would convince her. How embarrassing would it be to have to say, in front of an audience of millions, "Sorry, I wasn't able to get anything today."

She felt a whisper of air on her fingers and opened her eyes to see that Jaxx had hunched so far forward that her nose was almost on the crystal ball. "What can you see?"

Georgie took her hands away and saw the gently swirling white mist that presaged a message of some kind. She glanced again at Jaxx, curious about whether she could see it too. One look at her face was enough to know that she could. Her mouth dropped open very slightly, and when she looked up at Georgie, her eyes were a little wider. "What's that misty white stuff?"

"I don't really know. It just appears—although not everyone can see it," Georgie told her. "Sssh. Be very quiet for a moment, and I'll see what I can pick up."

A tiny frown came and went on Jaxx's face at being told to hush, but she pressed her lips together prettily and adopted an expression of tense antic-ipation.

The mist in the crystal ball slowly began to darken. It turned the color of heavy storm clouds and then began to spin.

And in the middle of it, Georgie could see the form of a woman running. Pursued.

Jaxx.

Oh, hell. She couldn't tell her *that.*

Find it at your preferred bookstore or online:
https://books2read.com/In-Good-Hands